TIME IS UP

BY

J. MICHAEL O'CONNOR

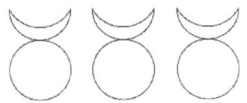

TIME IS UP

VOLUME III

The sequel to No Time Limit

Volume I

And

Time for change

Volume II

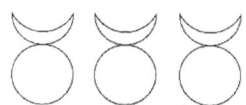

This book is dedicated to:

My beloved son, Sean Patrick O'Connor

12.20.1976-10.02.2007

My adoring Twin-flame,

Christine Jane O'Connor

The smile that brightens my day

03.22.1951-11.25.2014

Thank you, Sharon Clevinger, for prodding me into becoming the story taller.

A special thank you to Melissa J. for assisting me in the graphics.

copyright © 2023 J. Michael O'Connor

ISBN: 978-1-959700-08-1

J. Michael O'Connor

CHAPTERS

J. Michael O'Connor

Time Is Up

Tracking O'Francis

As a good journalist, friend, and "Brother," I tracked O'Francis in his new "educational" position. James P. had worked his new job as a homebound instructor for two years and had not had one complaint. No parents, no principals, no visits from Marshy's "Schutzstaffel troops."

Jim had gone the "extra mile" for the students he had to teach on their home turf and had gone that extra mile with the supervisors he had to mingle with in and around the central office from time to time. "Adapt and overcome," he would say. Of course, he was not entirely at ease in and around several of them, but for the most part, he was not under any stress and was enjoying his job for the first time in many years.

James P. was not teaching large groups in a classroom, but he learned to enjoy the one-on-one instruction he could give his homebound students. He knew they did not want good creative-minded teachers in any classroom, especially those making learning fun. He quickly found that he enjoyed the freedom of being out of the confines of a classroom.

However, he also realized he had been in a box— something he did not like.

James P. O'Francis also found being away from so many that had no desire to learn was a relief. He enjoyed being away from the ignorant bitching parents on some form of welfare, complaining about how hard he was and how much work he put on their "kid," or the affluent who expected special treatment for their "kid."

"Kid," a word which I learned that he hated. A "kid," he told me once when I used the term referring to students/children, is a fucking goat! A student is a child or children. I never made that mistake again.

James P. and Rebecca French, his "new" supervisor, once a foremost nemesis in his life, worked well together, to the surprise of most all in the central office.

Jim did the job he had been assigned, and she let him perform it in his way. It was possible that in his first two years, she just might have seen that he was not what she thought or what she had heard.

However, Jim had no illusions about her or anyone else he worked directly with or for. After all, he knew he was in the center of the viper pit. So he stepped very carefully. James P. had nothing for any one of the central office staff except for the ladies who did most of the work and kept the entire system operating. Rarely if ever, did they get any credit for their jobs. He liked them. Of course, he told me he never knew if it was all dissembling on their part. Trust for James P. was measured at zero. Jim was labeled a rogue by most teachers throughout the county.

Few knew the man he was. However, the ones who followed the "Fuhrer's" orders to the letter tainted James Patrick O'Francis' reputation and character and slandered his name throughout the Reynolds county school system and beyond would receive their just reward in due time.

The reward his nemesis had earned would be when they least expected it. Time was irrelevant for the avenger.

Homebound

It was now August, and it had been six months since the unfortunate events at the Alternative Education building occurred. At 3:00 A.M., he was still awake, listening to the sounds of rain. He had retired for the night at 11:30 P.M. and had quickly gone to sleep only to be awakened at 1:00 A.M. by rolling thunder echoing through the mountains.

He lay in his bed beside his soulmate, looking at the ceiling and listening to Dawn breathe. For an hour, he tried to sleep, hoping that the sounds of rain would drive away the violent thoughts that permeated his mind. Their cat "LaLa" had joined Jim as she so often did, only on his side of the bed, and had curled up at Jim's abdomen and was purring to her little heart's content.

Jim drifted off to sleep during the soothing sounds of the rain, the purring, and his mental communications with his spirit guides.

It was seven in the morning, and James P. had been up long before the alarm had gone off. He had showered, shaved, dressed, and drank coffee while watching CNN news. He often felt that the producers would be more diverse and report more about world events. Still, it was better than Fox "News," which he considered a propaganda network for the right wing evangelical GOP. But CNN, MSNBC, Reuters, and Sky were the only way he could keep up with world events. Moreover, he felt at least they made an honest effort to report the truth.

By eight in the morning, he met with John S. Marshall, his attorney, in an office inside the courthouse.

After reviewing instructions for courtroom procedures and how John Marshall expected James P. to act or not react to what he was about to go through, they went directly to the courtroom and took a seat.

By 10:00 A.M., he had witnessed several cases that he thought were relatively trivial to have been taking up the time of Juvenile Judge James M. Madison.

Judge Madison was forty-two years old and a native of Reynolds County. He had short-cropped hair of salt and pepper color with a neatly trimmed mustache which had not begun the change to salt. He wore round wire-rimmed glasses and a Masonic ring on his right hand and a wedding band on his left. His wife, Jim had learned, was also a teacher in the same county.

A brief conversation ensued between Judge Madison and John Jay, the Assistant Commonwealth Attorney assigned to the case by the Commonwealth Attorney Mark Bosch, whom Jim knew because of the political machine. He had to be elected to the position, and Jim had not only voted for him but had campaigned for him because he knew him as a Mason and knew him to be an honorable person.

Judge Madison looked around the courtroom for a few moments, then spoke sternly and clear.

"This next case will require a closed hearing. Anyone not connected to the Commonwealth versus James Patrick O'Francis must leave the courtroom."

April in the mountains was fresh with blooms on the trees, and the early flowers of tulips and daffodils brightened the landscape. It was a good warm spring morning and O'Francis had been invited to have lunch with the Alternative Education personnel. He would be finished with his morning student and would have a brief break before meeting with his afternoon student. His spirits were high, and he looked forward to socializing with the teachers and the director he had to work with from time to time.

Tracy Short was a thirty-five-year-old teacher's aide with dark Native American skin, dark hair, and dark eyes. Most would consider her beautiful. She was very well proportioned, stood five foot four, and weighed one hundred and twenty-five pounds.

Alicia Hoyden was a special education teacher in her late twenties and a former student from Honsburg High; she had black hair, was very attractive, still not married, and was a health enthusiast. She worked out at the local gym to keep her one-hundred-and-ten-pound body in perfect shape.

Linda Hawkins was the assistant director of the Alternative Program. She was fifty-five years old, a little overweight but acceptable for her age. Linda had a good personality, talked all the time, was very knowledgeable about various topics, and was a staunch Democrat. She had a happy laugh, and on the surface, she appeared to like Jim, and often over the past two years, they would discuss the good and bad of the school system and the politics involved in the system. For the most part, they agreed with each other. However, a little bit of a whisper from Jim's little voice kept him on alert when he was around her or dealing with any school/student issues.

Steward Brittin was the director of the program. He was a rather large man, a bit overweight, as was shown in his gut. However, his six-foot-five height did allow him to carry his excess weight a little better. Steward spoke with a deep voice. The kind one would have expected from a hard-core drill sergeant. His sixty-year-old body and facial features had not suffered a decline in appearance. His hair was not entirely white but maintained a good portion of its brown tone. He was a very intricate part of the political machine of Reynolds County.

Jim's connection to Steward went back many years, and he was well aware of his political power in the county. However, Jim knew he did not fit into that circle of elites.

There were times that Jim did not know whether to believe Steward or not as he was very much the politician, but he would play the game he was entrenched in and hoped he did not make any fatal mistakes.

As one entered the courtroom, James Patrick was sitting at the very end of a ten-foot-long dark, wooden, much-worn pew in the front row. The benches extended some fifteen rows deep with an aisle way separating the same number of benches to his left. He figured this was done to separate the warring parties at any one time having to be in the courtroom.

Directly in the center of the aisle at the front of the courtroom, three steps higher than the main floor level, the Judge sat behind his six-foot-wide and three-foot-deep dark wooden podium. A witness chair was directly in front of the judge's podium, one step up from the courtroom floor, with a rail separating the bench pews from the witness chair. A railing separated the attorneys about ten feet from the judge, and each attorney had a large wooden table six feet by two feet with two office chairs covered in brown cloth.

As O'Francis looked around the courtroom, he saw four other people remaining in the room, including Bruce McCloud, the alleged victim.

John Marshall instructed Jim to join him at his table. As he looked directly across the room to the prosecuting side of the courtroom, a young John Jay was seated, arranging his papers in some order, preparing himself for his case.

He was a good-looking young man: six-foot-tall, one hundred and eight pounds, wearing wire round-rimmed glasses.

Jim wondered to himself if the round wire-rimmed glasses were an attorney thing. He had short brown hair parted in the middle, with a dark blue suit, a white shirt, and a dark blue tie. He wore a wedding band on his left hand and a Mason ring on his right.

Then his eyes traveled beyond the Assistant Prosecuting Attorney to the one pew that sat behind John Jay. There seated on the bench were two social workers: a man he did not know and the female that sat beside him. Jim's eyes narrowed with hardness as he looked at the female. *Just two more members of the Marshy "Schutzstaffel," he thought.*

After taking the next two days off work from his encounter at the A.E. school with Bruce, Jim went to his office. He spent the weekend reliving the events and putting them down on paper for documentation for his supervisor.

On Monday, he returned to work, hand-delivered the report to Ms. Rebecca French, and went about his job going from one student's house to another.

He had worked for two days to put the events into some perspective and put them behind him.

The only really good thing about the day as he entered his office, it was Wednesday, "hump" day as the working world referred to it. Jim felt tired and was in an ill mood because of the lack of sleep—re-living the attack by a student. In addition, he had been fighting a series of not welcomed ghosts coming to visit that always seemed to leave him drained.

The light flashed on his answering machine, so he reached over and pushed the button as he set his coffee mug down on his desk.

"Mr. O'Francis, this is Rebecca. I need to see you as soon as you get into the office. Do not go to your regularly scheduled student before you talk to me."

Jim stood for a moment letting the message ramble through his mind, and then he spoke aloud to no one as if someone were in the room listening to him.

"Well, shit, this can't be good! I am in no mood for any buffalo chips being thrown at me today."

His eyes indicated his lack of sleep as they were bloodshot with dark shadows under them. He sat down at his desk for a moment and looked out of the window at the lush greening mountains far to the north and wished he were in them instead of where he was.

He then tried to become more positive in his thoughts and self-verbal conversation.

"Ahhh, maybe she has yet another student and most likely one more that is pregnant and needs to give me some inside information on the parents."

He got up, went out his door, and headed to Rebecca French's office. But the little voice in his head began sending him warnings that this would not be a good meeting.

Jim pecked on Rebecca's door and entered with a warm and friendly, "Good morning, Rebecca."

"Good morning, Jim. How are you today?"

"Ahhh, I am doing well under the circumstances, I guess. But, hey, crap happens in our business. We just got to adjust and move on. So, what's up?" His mind instantly flashed to his son's term of what's up as "SUP," and a smile crossed his face.

She had been sitting at the table behind her desk doing some paperwork, then pulled her seat back around to her office desk. She stated. "Mr. O'Francis, I have some bad news for you. Social Services have charged you with child abuse."

Jim continued to smile as he stood directly in front of her desk and then responded sarcastically, "Child abuse, right."

Rebecca was not smiling, nor did she give any hint of a practical joke on her face that Jim could detect.

"Jim, I am very serious. Someone called them and filed a complaint."

James Patrick kind of half-laughed.

"Look, Rebecca, this had better be a joke."

"I assure you, Jim, that it is not a joke. It is very serious. I have nothing for Social Service, and there are big problems anytime they get involved in the school business."

The warm smile Jim had adorned for only a few moments had now left, and an expressionless stone look graced his tired-looking face.

"Rebecca, I can assure you I have not abused anyone. So just whom does Social Services claim that I have abused? I mean, they must have me confused with someone else. Right?"

"Bruce McCloud," French stated.

"Who?" he responded as the name did not register as it was not on his list of the nine students he had on homebound.

"Bruce McCloud. Jim, the boy you had the altercation with at the Alternative Education Building a few days ago.

"Rebecca, there is no way. I mean, you read my report. It is supported by, by, ahh, Tracy Short. Rebecca, I did not lie. I told you the truth, all facts, and no fabrications."

"Jim, I believe you. I do. But what we have here is a bunch of Social Service idiots who are running amuck and doing what they want to any teacher they can get their fangs into to suck the blood out. They're assholes! Believe me, I know because I have dealt with them on several occasions in the past."

"Rebecca, I do not even know this...this piece of shit! No, shit can be used for good use... whatever he is...I cannot even come up with a word. He had no real purpose. I mean, this is a large pile of buffalo chips."

Jim then sat down very heavily in the chair to the left of Rebecca's desk. "Look, Rebecca, I really do not know who the hell these people are, but they have the wrong information. Child abuse! Great God

Almighty, I have not gotten my glasses back yet, which cost me two hundred dollars to repair. Now, who is going to pay for my loss? And I have been charged with child abuse. Damn, what kind of FUBAR do we have here?" He thought Rebecca did not know what the anagram stood for.

"You are correct. This is a FUBAR..., and yes, I know what it means."

"Who called Social Services anyway?" O'Francis inquired.

"I really don't know."

"Okay, well, think about it. I mean, there were just a few who could have. These few are in the Alternative Program, and there is..." he paused momentarily. "Who was it, Linda Hawkins?" Jim stated with a harsh tone and disgust in his voice.

"I mean, she thinks these little bastards are to be treated like all other students in our system. Hell, if that were the case, they would not be in alternative education now, would they? That is why they are where they are, for Christ's sake!"

Jim stopped venting and just looked at his supervisor. "Sorry I went off like that, Rebecca. It is not your fault. I have not been sleeping well lately, and I am just a little on edge."

"Jim, there is no need for an apology. I understand completely. It is a FUBAR, and the fact is that these people can do whatever they want, and we are at their mercy. Jim, believe me when I tell you they really like going after teachers. You have to give your testimony in front of a Social Service caseworker in two days, and she is a real bitch. I will set it up in the small conference room. I want you to call Dan Jakes and tell him to get John Marshall as your attorney. He is the best attorney in these matters."

James Patrick knew at that moment that it was an awful situation for Rebecca to tell him to place a call to Dan Jakes because he was the one person she had battled for years over school-related issues, and she had no love for him at all.

Jim rose from his chair. "I will do as you have instructed. Child abuse. Christ, Rebecca. Hell, I should have brought charges against him for assault and battery. He hit me, not the reverse. Damn."

O'Francis then went out the door, stopped, and returned quickly.

"I want to know who made the call to the Social Services. This is a school matter. Also, did Mr. Brittin do anything to the boy?"

"I am not sure."

"You are not sure? Have you talked to Mr. Brittin about what took place? I gave him the same detailed account of what took place."

"Yes, he and I talked briefly."

"And...?"

"He did not indicate that he would do anything to the boy."

"Well, now that tells you volumes."

Rebecca French did not respond to Jim's comment, and they just looked at each other for several seconds.

"Jim, I want you to go and make the call to Dan Jakes before you do anything else today. Trust me on this one. These people are totally ruthless."

O'Francis turned and went back to his office. Sitting for several minutes thinking before he called Dan, he reflected on Rebecca's last words.

Totally ruthless. What in the hell does she think La Mar and his SS troops have been doing over the past decade?

Jim knew that Rebecca had been part of that SS group herself. *Hell, I wonder if she thinks people have such a short memory that they do not remember what she has done to other teachers, including me. I wonder if she made the call and is trying to implicate the people at Alternative.*

Yet, Jim was taken aback by Rebecca's support of him. Something he did not expect and would have bet against. He was not sure if it was support or not—just covering her ass was more like it. He kept looking for the bullet coming toward his head.

O'Francis called Dan Jakes, and by that afternoon, he was in John Scott Marshall's law office telling him what had gone down and provided him with a copy of the documentation he had given to Rebecca French.

The lead Social Service investigator had connected with Linda Hawkins and Bruce McCloud's mother and had criminal charges brought against James Patrick for assault and battery.

Gavel Down

The door to the courtroom was closed, and the room was silent. Judge Madison then spoke.

"Is the Commonwealth ready?"

"Yes, your Honor." John Jay replied.

Jim's mid-section became as tight as a drum.

"Is the defense ready?"

"Yes, your Honor." John Marshall replied.

Judge Madison looked at Jim and stated,

"James Patrick O'Francis, the Commonwealth has charged you with assault and battery. How do you plead?"

Marshall leaned over to Jim and whispered in his right ear, "Not guilty."

"I plead not guilty, your Honor."

Looking back to his right, he addressed John Jay, "You may call your first witness."

John Jay called his first witness, a girl named Kelli Bartels.

Jim sat and listened to her version of what had taken place that day, and it did not sift out exactly how it actually went down. John Marshall took his time getting up for his cross exam of Kelli Bartels.

"Tell me, Miss Bartels. Did you see Mr. O'Francis hit Bruce McCloud?"

"No," was her response.

"Did you see Bruce hit Mr. O'Francis?"

"Yes."

"Miss Bartels, you stated that you saw Mr. O'Francis put his hands around Bruce's neck. Is that correct?"

"Yes."

"Was Mr. McCloud turning blue?"

"I don't understand what you mean."

"Well, Miss Bartels, if you saw Mr. O'Francis choking Bruce, he would be cutting off his air supply. Therefore, he would not be breathing. Now, was he gasping for air?"

"Well, no, not really."

"Okay, Miss Bartels, was Bruce talking or saying anything while Mr. O'Francis had him by the throat as you have testified here today?"

"Ahhh, I think so. I am not for sure. But he was choking Bruce. So Mr. O'Francis just grabbed Bruce by the throat which started the fight."

"Was he using any foul language while all this was happening?"

"Well... yeah."

"Miss Bartels, after the altercation occurred, what happened then?"

"Well, Mrs. Hawkins came in and took Mr. O'Francis out of the room."

"How did she do this?"

"Well, she got in front of him and pushed him backward out of the room."

"Did Mr. O'Francis resist?"

"Well, no, I don't think so."

"Where did all the students go after all this took place?"

"Well, all the teachers went into one of the offices and put all of us in a classroom."

"So you are stating that every one of the students was in a classroom by yourselves just after the altercation between Bruce McCloud and Mr. O'Francis had occurred."

"Yes."

"Were any teachers in the room with you and the rest of the students?"

"No."

"Were there any teachers' aides present?"

"No."

"Was Bruce McCloud in the same room with the rest of the students?"

"Well, yeah, he is a student, too."

John Marshall went back to the table and picked up a written statement Bartels had given to the social worker. He turned around toward the witness with the paper in his hand. "Miss Bartels, you had stated that you heard Bruce McCloud tell Mr. O'Francis that his father had been killed in an automobile accident and that you heard Mr. O'Francis say, 'So.' Now I ask you, where were you sitting when this conversation took place?"

"Well, I was across the room at my table."

"Was Mr. O'Francis facing you when he had this conversation with Bruce?"

"No, he was looking at Bruce."

"So, is it possible that you misunderstood what Mr. O'Francis said? Yes or no?"

"I don't think so. I heard him say, 'So.' That is when Bruce got all mad and started cussing Mr. O'Francis, and he just went after Bruce."

"Miss Bartels, answer the question yes or no. Could you have misunderstood Mr. O'Francis?"

"No."

"Miss Bartels, could Mr. O'Francis have said 'Oh,' instead of 'So'?"

Kelli Bartels paused before she answered and looked at John Marshall. "I am sure. I mean, I thought he said, 'So.'"

"Did Mr. O'Francis cuss Mr. McCloud?"

"No."

"How far away would you say you were sitting when this conversation took place?"

"Across the room."

"I understand that, Miss Bartels, but give me a guess. How many feet would you say you were from Mr. O'Francis?"

She began looking around the room... "Ahhh, oh, maybe from here to the wall over there." Kelli pointed toward the left side wall from the witness stand.

"So you would guess that you were, oh, let's say, about thirty feet, would that sound about right?"

"Yeah, I guess. Ever how far that is."

John Marshall turned to the judge. "That is all I have at this time, your Honor."

The other two witnesses testified, and all had the same exact story, including Bruce McCloud, who played the humble, poor, little heartbroken boy over the loss of his father.

But what did not come out in the case was that he and his father did not get along, and they had come to physical blows from time to time. It also did not come out that Bruce had even become physically violent with his mother, that Bruce and Rhymes, his best friend in the alternative school, both were drug users and had begun the process of being dealers in the small town in which they hung out.

Jim knew all this but knew that bringing it to the surface would only make his defense look as if he was attacking the character of the heartbroken boy who had lost his "beloved father."

After going through all the witnesses, Jim was called to the stand and testified to the events that occurred late in April. After being cross-examined with a good deal of intensity by John Jay, he informed the judge that the prosecution rested its case.

Jim was pleased with how his attorney had defended him. He now sat straight in his chair and watched the judge as he pondered the case's evidence before him.

After five minutes of silence in the room, Judge Madison briefly reviewed the case and presented all the testimony. Jim's gut tightened as he listened to what the judge was saying.

He tried to keep a positive attitude about the case. However, it appeared that the judge was leaning in favor of the prosecution. In addition, he knew that the witnesses and Bruce McCloud had lied about what had happened.

He knew that all the students had made up what they would say and had stuck together with their stories.

Jim had little faith in the judicial system and feared that the judge would believe the act the role of the good little students and the terrible teacher who had just walked into their little world and attacked one of their own without cause.

James Patrick knew this was the one area that would put the nail in his coffin with the superintendent and the School Board. If he lost this case, it would mean that his career as a teacher was over. He feared what the verdict would be. However, his greatest fear was the damage to his character and what it would mean to his name.

He sat stone-still with no expression as Judge Madison came to a close of the facts presented to him.

"I have considered all testimonies in this case, and I believe that even though Mr. O'Francis should have never used such language in the presence of a student, he was not the one who provoked the attack by Mr. McCloud and was defending himself from his attacker. Therefore, I find in favor of the defendant Mr. O'Francis. He is innocent of the charges of assault and battery. Therefore he is free to go."

Judge Madison brought his gavel down hard, echoing throughout the courtroom. "This court is adjourned."

Jim remained motionless as Judge Madison rose, took a quick glance toward Jim, and went out the door to the rear of the courtroom. The court stenographer Kathy Faye, seated to the judge's right, rose, paused just momentarily, looked over at Jim, and broke just the slightest of a smile. O'Francis looked across at the Assistant Commonwealth Attorney, who was looking at Jim. John Jay then broke a slight smile, picked up his papers, put them in his briefcase, and closed the lid.

Jim rose and faced John Marshall.

"Thank you so very much. Believe me when I tell you this. For the first time in a long time, I was afraid that I was about to lose not just my job with the loss of this case but my character as a person."

John Marshall smiled from ear to ear.

"You doubted me? Why Jim? I am shocked. Jim, this case had no merit. Judge Madison knew they were lying, as did John Jay, but they had to go through the process. You had some very powerful people on your side today, but I think you know that. I do have one question for you. Do you know Ms. Faye, the court stenographer?"

"Kind of. I had her son and daughter in one of my classes some years ago."

"Hmm, okay, anyway now, we still have to deal with Social Services."

"I do not understand. I thought this was it."

John laughed as he placed his files into his briefcase. "Oh no, Jim, not by a long shot. Social Service will come after you with a vengeance. They have laws with which our court system has nothing to do with. And that woman across the room is not very happy if you have not noticed."

"But John, the law is the law, and I have been acquitted of all the charges, correct?"

"Yes, you have been acquitted of all charges brought against you in a court of law. But as I stated, Social Services has its own laws, and our legal system does not govern them. But do not worry, we will get through all that in time."

Spoiled

Damon Bales walked into the central office of the Reynolds County School System in an angry and disturbed state of mind.

A dark silver van pulled into the far end of the Food City parking lot one hundred and fifty yards away as the "crow flies" from the office of the superintendent's side of the building. The driver parked the van, turned off the engine, exited the driver's side, then closed and locked the door. Next, he walked around to the van's right side and put his thumb on the spot over the concaved handle. It clicked (a separate lock from the driver/passenger doors.) Next, he opened the sliding door. The cargo section of the van had no windows, and he reached to his right to a custom-made wall behind the driver's and passenger's seats and flipped a switch that lit a dim light on the ceiling of the cargo section.

The floor of the cargo section was covered with indoor and outdoor light gray carpet. The area had two comfortable office chairs bolted to the floor, one on each side of the van. The right side chair was toward the front, and the left side chair was toward the back. The walls were filled with a wide selection of high-tech, state-of-the-art electronic equipment, monitors, and taping equipment, with a table two feet wide extending from the front of the cargo section to the back doors, gracing both sides of the cargo section. The rear doors had been welded together, and the back door section of the van had custom-made shelves installed. Note tablets hung from hooks on the front edges of the tables. Pens and pencils were placed in cups in circular holes cut out of several places on the tops of the table.

He sat in the van's right side chair and began to flip switches to eavesdropping electronics. On top of the van, a dish-shaped sphere was elevated. Then, at its pinnacle of two feet, it stopped, and another bright silver sphere began to unfold. When it stopped, a pencil-shaped rod began to extend outward for eighteen inches and stopped. The sphere rotated to where the rod was pointed toward Marshy's office.

Inside the van, a reel-to-reel tape began to turn as *"the man"* placed a set of earphones over his ears.

"Good morning. My name is Damon Bales, and I want to see Mr. Marshy," as Damon Bales harshly addressed the receptionist.

"Mr. Bales, do you have an appointment?"

"No."

"I will see if Mr. Marshy will see you."

"He will." His tone of voice was curt and demanding.

She picked up the phone and pushed a button.

"Mr. Marshy, a Mr. Bales is here and wants to talk to you."

"Do I have an appointment with him?" La Mar asked. As Grace looked over at Damon, who had taken several steps from the receptionist's desk, she answered, "No, sir. I do not have one on the appointment sheet. Mr. Marshy, Mr. Gardner is coming in today at ten o'clock."

"Okay, send him in." She placed the phone down and looked up at Bales.

"You may go back. Just..."

Bales rudely cut her off. "I know where it is!"

Damon Bales walked out of the lobby to the circular hallway, turned left, and quickly walked to Marshy's office on the backside of the building facing the Food City's parking lot. He entered the secretary's office, went by Sally without speaking, entered Marshy's enormous thirty feet by forty-foot office, and closed the door behind him.

"Well, Damon, come in." La Mar did not get out of his chair. His desk is set in the middle of the quarter moon-shaped room. Two tan leather chairs were placed at the front on each side of his desk. "Have a seat, Damon."

"What in the hell is going on!" Bales sternly stated.

"What do you mean?" Marshy replied.

"I mean with that goddamn O'Francis!"

"Hell, Damon, I don't know. What are you talking about? You come storming in here mad as a wet hen and demand the answer to a question I don't know what you are talking about."

"Damn it, La Mar, I am talking about the trial! So you mean you don't know that he got off on the assault and battery charges!"

"Yes. I am very much aware of this fact. So?"

"So! So! Hell, how did he do that?"

"He had a good attorney?" Marshy stated with a smile.

Damon sat red-faced at Marshy's smart-ass remark. "Well, Damon, you were the one who told me that you could get Judge MacMullur to get Judge Madison to convict him. What more can I say?"

"Well, La Mar, you told me you would get political pressure on Madison. What the hell happened to that?"

"I did my best. I can't go to Madison and tell him how to rule on a case. I do have limits, you know. You were the one who seemed so convinced that he would rule to convict. If he had, we could recommend that the board dismiss O'Francis as a teacher. But, Damon, it didn't work. So don't get your shorts in a squeeze."

"God damn it! That sonofabitch! How does he keep getting off?" Marshy grinned.

"So, what is so damn funny, La Mar?"

"I thought you didn't like the word son of a bitch?"

"Ahh, fuck you, La Mar!"

"Well, you were the one who wanted him fired for calling you a son of a bitch, not me."

"So, now what?"

"Well, he still has to face charges of child abuse. The Social Services Board will have a hearing on that sometime soon. So we will see what happens there."

"You have connections there," Bales asked.

"Yes," La Mar stated.

"And?" Bales replied.

"I have made in-roads. We will see."

The phone rang. Marshy reached over and picked it up. "Yes."

Grace, the receptionist, spoke, "Mr. Marshy, your ten o'clock appointment is here."

"Okay, give me a few minutes." Then Marshy laid the phone down on the receiver. "Look, Damon, I have someone I have to talk to. Calm down. Things will work out."

Damon got up, still agitated, turned, and walked out of Marshy's office.

The man in the van spoke softly, "Very good."

O'Donovan

I want to take you back a few years in my story about O'Francis. This was not the first time Jim had to be in court, a legal system in which he lacked faith because of its corruption. He talked to me shortly after the trial, thanked me for being present, and in our conversation, we rehashed the events that led him to distrust the legal system.

Although O'Francis' "will" appearance is like steel, and it seemed that he could endure anything, I had doubts about how long the "steel well" in him would last under his current stress and pressure.

Over my life, I have learned that by covering one story after another, humans can only take so much. Then when you least expect it, they come apart, usually at their demise, leaving a destroyed family with questions that can never be answered.

But Jim was different, and as I have stated in my story, he is one that I do not believe I will ever come across again. What I uncovered on my own with the help of Jim, I still do not know how he could obtain such covert information. However, I believe there is someone else in his life to whom he has never made any reference that provided him with such detailed secret information. This leads me to think that this other person has some governmental connection, which does not surprise me, considering the kind of people Jim was once connected with.

As a good journalist should, on several occasions I inquired where the information he was passing along to me was obtained and its validity in telling my story. Of course, after fact-checking, the data always proved to be correct. But, as I expected, I got no answers about his source or sources. But this is not taking you back to the mid-nineties when he lost faith in our legal system. So I fully understand why O'Francis ended up the way he did.

The Clerk

Jermaine picked up the phone and dialed the number of Damon Bales. After three rings, the connection was made.

"Hello," Damon said.

"Damon, this is Jermaine. I need to speak with you. Can you come by my house tonight, say about seven?"

"Why?"

"Well, I don't want to talk on the phone. It is important."

"I guess." Then there was a long pause.

"It's about your case," Jermaine stated.

"Say at seven?" Damon said.

"Yeah."

"Okay, I'll be there."

Damon arrived at Jermaine's house on time. They went to Jermaine's den and sat in two oversized, well-padded, high-backed chairs. Jermaine had provided iced tea to drink as they talked.

"So, what is new?" Damon started the conversation.

"I have this juror that we can reach. Well, kind of. Let me explain what I have in mind."

Damon smiled. His blood rushed through his veins at such a speed it warmed his whole body.

"Okay, a little "under-the-table" money. He tells the judge that O'Francis tried to bribe him."

"This is great. Are you sure he will cooperate?"

"Yes, I am sure. Damon."

Graft

Damon Bales had Richard Finkel come by his house, which was extremely rare, as Damon did not feel that Richard was in his league of players.

When Richard arrived at Damon's house, it was midday on a warm Sunday. Damon took him to his back patio area where he had laid out some finger foods and a pitcher of iced tea.

He wasted no time in getting to the point of the meeting. He informed Richard of Jermaine Griffith's and his plan, which he called our insurance policy.

After informing Finkel that they would have to come up with ten grand to be distributed among several key players in the forthcoming trial, Richard was skeptical if the money was worth it. It was a gamble.

Damon got a bit agitated at Richard. "So you are running a betting operation out of the AD's office and are unwilling to bet on a sure thing."

"Well, Damon, how do you know it is a sure bet?" Richard countered.

Again, Damon did not reveal all his "cards" to Richard. "Because, Richard, I know. Leave it at that. It is not that you cannot handle five grand."

Richard drank his tea, picked up a triangle-cut tuna sandwich, and looked at Bales. He ate the half tuna sandwich, took a sip of tea, and then stated. "Let me get this straight, two judges: Janice Jones and Joan Dobson..."

Damon interrupted him, "Don't forget Gerry and Bankos."

"Damon, you will not get either one of them to testify on our behalf. I know. You will have to trust me on this one. So, Damon, where does Janice fit into all this?"

"Oh, I brought her in on our case because she will testify that O'Francis has terrorized her and Gil for years. That will establish a pattern. That is why I sent the letter to law enforcement and the judges."

Richard just looked at Damon. Several seconds passed.

"You sent letters to exactly whom. I thought the letter was going to the school board and Mr. Marshy."

"Look, Richard. First, Janice is good at what she does. Second, she can be convincing to a jury. As to the distribution of the letter, well, I figured if the law enforcement knew how dangerous O'Francis was, it would also support what Janice will testify to."

"Damon, you did keep this letter local, correct?" Richard's voice had a concerning tone to it.

"All except one. Janice told me she had called the FBI on a couple of occasions and reported the acts of terror on them, so I sent one to the FBI."

"Fuck, Damon. Really, I mean the fucking FBI! You actually believed her. I mean, really. Shit! Do you or does one of your political buds have an agent in your pocket? I mean, man, you don't fuck with the Feds! Damnit! The fucking Feds!"

There were several minutes of silence as Richard calmed down.

"Okay, so, just how are we distributing this money? I mean, look, this shit is dangerous. If we are..." Damon cut Richard off.

"Let me take care of how much each gets and how they will receive it." But, again, Bales did not reveal all the cards to Richard.

The insurance plan was set in motion on a sunny church-going Sunday midday.

The Trial

Michael O'Francis had taken off work and traveled six hours to be with his family for the trial. All three men in the O'Francis family wore double-breasted blue pinstriped suits, light blue button-down collared shirts, and highly shined black shoes. They met Julius Donatello at the courthouse. It was thirty minutes before the trial was to begin. Julius had a box of files he was carrying.

They entered the courtroom taking their seats on the left side of the judge's chair. Dawn, Michael, and Patrick sat on the first row behind the rail on the same side as Jim and Julius. The room was filled with oak-colored, pew-like benches divided into two sections—the aisle separating the two rows of thirty pews. The railing was three feet high, with spindles separating the top and bottom. A gate swung forward and backward at the center of the aisle. The witness stand sat in the center, one step up from the floor level. It was a box shape with a chair inside and an opening that faced the judge and the jury section. The judge's lofty position was overlooking the jurors below him and looking over the rest of the courtroom.

The prosecution and the defending side had a six-foot oak-colored table and three wooden chairs.

Across from Jim and Julius were Richard, Damon, and their attorney, Curtis Feinstein. Jim did not hesitate in looking at all three with utter contempt. Their posture depicted smugness and confidence. Julius was placing his files on the table in front of O'Francis.

Jim noted that Julius had not brought the poster he had requested that illustrated the incidences showing Damon's pattern of harassment and character assassination of James P.

Manuel and Nina Reuben entered the courtroom and sat at the back of the room on the side of Jim's family. Both had been at Jim and Dawn's side supporting them in every way. They understood the corruption and the character assassination by Marshy's loyal legions. Emmanuel had suffered through the harassment, the deceit, and the threats by several of Marshy's "SS" troops.

Also sitting in the back on the opposite side of the room was John O'Donovan, and the late arrival was Paul O'Neill.

Jim observed that John wore casual attire, and Paul wore a suit. The two did not know each other and sat in separate pews.

He also noted that a reporter from the newspaper was present, dressed in casual attire that appeared as if he had slept in them all night. He knew him from the many times he had been at the School Board meetings. His accounts of the School Board meetings always seemed to portray La Mar and "company" in glorious heavenly light, and the teachers' association seemed to be the villains.

On several occasions, the teachers' association's president questioned the reporter about the manner and accuracy in which he had reported what had taken place at the School Board meeting. As usual, he responded with a sarcastic answer. Jim figured that he was at the trial upon the request of Marshy to portray him in the worst manner possible and portray Bales and Finkel as the poor victims.

Dan Jakes was a no-show. Instead, Jim logged it away as yet another lesson in support and importance of the game he was now playing, as well as, maybe he did not know Dan as well as he may have thought.

Two county police officers, Charles Kuntz and James Fleming, entered the courtroom. Jim knew both men well. The judge entered the room moments later, and Charles Kuntz announced his presence.

"All rise." He spoke loud and clear, "The honorable Dan Munis presiding."

"Be seated," Charles stated as Judge Munis took his seat. Jim told me once that he never did like that ritual.

"That is a throwback to England and their fucked up kingship system."

The court clerk read the case number, what the case was about, and who brought the suit.

"Is the defense ready?" Judge Munis asked.

"Yes, your honor," came the response from Curtis Feinstein.

"Is the plaintiff ready?" he asked.

"Yes, your honor," Julius stated.

"Will the clerk call in the juror pool?" Judge Munis stated.

With those instructions, the court clerk, Jermaine Griffith, went to the back of the courtroom, went out the large walnut-colored double door and returned with fifteen people, of which five would be picked for the trial.

As the men and women took their seats, Jermaine Griffith announced to Judge Munis that he had been informed that Mr. O'Francis had contacted one of the jurors.

Judge Munis asked which one.

"Your Honor, Mr. Brian Weber," Jermaine announced.

"How?" Judge Munis asked.

"Your honor, according to Mr. Weber, Mr. O'Francis had learned he was scheduled to be part of the jury pool and went to his place of employment, Food City, and spoke with him concerning this case."

The judge looks down and over at Jim and Julius.

Julius turned his head toward Jim. "Do you know this person?"

"No."

"Did you talk to him at any time?"

"No," Jim stated with a harsh tone in his voice.

"Are you sure?" Julius asked again.

Jim looked directly into Julius' eyes. His eyes were cold and without feeling.

"I said no! That statement is a goddamn lie! And Julius, I expect more of such lies as the day goes on! Just like there was when your sister questioned them in the deposition. I have tried to tell you that there is not a low level these fucking people will not go to. I told all of you that they had no honor and integrity!"

"Mr. Weber, is the person named in the courtroom?"

Weber answered yes.

"Can you point the person out?"

Weber stated, "Yes, Sir," and pointed toward Jim.

"Mr. Weber, you are excused. You may leave." Judge Munis stated.

Damon smiled and leaned back in his seat, crossing his arms over his chest.

At that point, James Patrick knew that the die was cast. Instilling in the minds of whatever jurors were picked, he would be viewed differently. A cold chill raced over his body, leaving "goosebumps" over his back and arms.

The two attorneys would strike or accept as the clerk called each name. The process took the better part of the morning until they had the five required for a civil suit.

To the left of Dawn, Michael, and Patrick was Mr. Lucius Donatello, Julius' father. Jim had requested that Holly be part of the team at his table. He wanted her to question Damon. He knew that she could bring the worst out in him, as he hated any female who held a professional position, could not be controlled, and had power over him. She was not present. For Jim, this was a significant disappointment. He began to feel very uneasy and a bit angry. On the other side of the room were his current wife, Damon, and several members of the Honsburg community that did not have honorable reputations. Bales' autocratic rule in high school created a cult following, and they remained loyal and supported him.

The knowledge Jim had gained about the people in the community and his colleagues and their dissembling did not surprise him to see them present in support of Damon and Richard.

Julius Donatello then stood and delivered his opening statement to the jury.

"Ladies and gentlemen of the jury, this trial is about character assassination. It is about slander, it is about libel, and it is about defaming the character of one Mr. James Patrick O'Francis. This case is about Mr. Bales and Mr. Finkel conspiring to destroy my client's reputation. This case is about a letter that Mr. Bales wrote and sent to the Reynolds County School Board in hopes that they would fire Mr. O'Francis from a job he has held in this county for over twenty years. Instead, Mr. Bales fired him from his coaching job, which provided ten percent of his family's income, placing them under a financial burden." Julius walked from one side of the five jurors to the other and continued with his opening.

"Mr. Bales has not provided any solid proof of why Mr. O'Francis was dismissed from his coaching position which he has held for thirteen years. Mr. O'Francis was a well-respected coach among his coaching colleagues, opponents, and officials overseeing the games he was involved in. Mr. Bales has not provided any evidence that has proven otherwise. Mr. Bales went one step further. He sent a copy of this defaming letter to all law enforcement agencies throughout the entire area, including the FBI, to cast a dark cloud over Mr. O'Francis, labeling him as a terrorist."

Julius finished by defining some keywords enabling the jurors to understand their meanings fully.

Curtis Feinstein sprang up like a jack-in-a-box just as Julius' ass hit the seat. He told the jurors that Bales had been damaged—informing them that his client Damon C. Bales had lived in fear for five years. Curtis made his opinion passionate. Repeating the fact, his client had been living in fear. He would raise his voice each time he uttered the phrase "living in fear," expressing to the five jurors the emotion of what "fear" Damon had been living with. Curtis's performance was as if he were performing for a packed house audience in the Kennedy Center. Curtis Feinstein portrayed Jim as not just a simple teacher. He was more than that. He was not what he appeared, as he reiterated several times.

Jim listened to each word, phrase, and line of his theatric performance, and as he finally concluded, Jim thought, *"You have no fucking idea what I could do if I release the abilities I have in bondage. You stupid mother-fucker! Bales and his cronies are fortunate I love my family more than my loathing for you."*

Julius began to call his first witness, Mr. George Rake.

"Your honor," Mr. Feinstein rose quickly and spoke. "I do not have this witness on my list."

Jim looked over at Julius. Julius quickly rose.

"Your honor, I have provided the clerk with all my witnesses, including Mr. Rake. Mr. Feinstein should have received this list."

"Approach. You too, Mr. Griffith." Judge Munis stated. Feinstein, Donatello, and Griffith went to the Judge.

"Mr. Feinstein, would you care to explain?"

"Yes, sir. I do not have Mr. Rake on my list."

"Your honor," Julius stated. "I have provided the clerk and Mr. Feinstein with a list of all the people I intend to call as witnesses."

"Do you have a list of people you intend to call?"

"Yes, sir." Julius quickly returned to the table, picked up his list of witnesses, and handed the judge the list.

"And you, Mr. Feinstein." Judge Munis asked.

"Yes." Already having the list in his hand, he handed over his list. Judge Munis looked at both lists.

"Gentlemen, we seem to have some problems with communications here. Mr. Donatello, your list does not match the one Mr. Feinstein has. Mr. Griffith, do you have a list of people both parties will call in this case?"

"Yes, your honor." Griffith had the list and was ready to present it to the judge. Jim thought it was strange to have the list of witnesses prepared for the judge to review. Griffith handed the judge his list. Munis looked at the list.

"Mr. Donatello, Mr. Griffith's list does not match yours. Four people on your list don't appear on Mr. Griffith's or Mr. Feinstein's."

"Your honor, I really don't understand. I am sure I provided each with the list of witnesses I intended to call."

"Well, I can't allow these people to be called as witnesses." He placed checkmarks beside the names and handed the list back to Julius.

"If you would like to reschedule this case for a later date, we can. Or would you like to continue with the people you have?" Judge Munis was cold and unfeeling in his tone of voice.

"I will confer with my client, your Honor."

"You may step back," Judge Munis stated.

Julius walked back to the table where Jim was seated.

"We have a slight problem." Jim did not respond. He just looked at Julius with no surprise on his face. He expected glitches in the case, as there had been over the past five years of just getting the lawsuit trial scheduled.

"It seems that our witness list is incomplete. They do not have all of our witnesses listed. Therefore, the judge will not allow us to use these four as witnesses."

Jim looked down at the list of key people in his case: *Greg Roscommon,* Athletic Director and teaching colleague. He knew of some of Damon's underhanded tactics toward Jim and would have been very open and trustful in answering any questions.

Steward Brittin was a well-known, influential member of the Democratic political machine in the county, who was willing to testify (Jim and Julius thought) to Damon's character and that Damon Bales was well known throughout the county for his character assassination and dislike for O'Francis. He was also willing to testify to several conversations where Damon openly and blatantly slandered Jim when he was present.

Dave Hobart, head football coach at Honsburg High School, would testify, although not so willingly, but would tell the truth if asked about conversations he had with Richard Finkel that were demeaning to Jim and his son Michael.

Belinda Bookman, secretary at Honsburg High, had been there since Jim arrived and knew of and had seen and heard Bales and Finkel discrediting Jim.

O'Francis looked up at the judge, now looking toward Jim and Julius. The courtroom was deadly silent. Jim then slowly turned toward the clerk, leaning against the far wall directly across from him and behind Damon's table. Jermaine Griffith had a smirk expression on his face.

Damon leaned back in his chair with a smile on his face. Feinstein was looking across at Julius, waiting to see what he would do.

"Do you want to continue with what we have? Or do you want to get the trial put off until later?"

James Patrick knew at that moment the case was doomed. He knew it was useless to postpone the trial, and what he now felt in every part of his body was a corrupt system of so-called justice.

It would be a waste of his time and his money. The cards were stacked. It was crunch time. The bases were loaded. There were two outs in the bottom of the ninth inning. He had to swing away and hope for a hit to win the game. His mind was racing. It appeared that everything was going in slow motion.
The room remained deadly silent.

Jim looked first at his attorney and then across the room at his enemies. He slowly turned his head and looked at John and Paul diagonally to the far back of the courtroom. He paused for several seconds while looking at them. They returned the look, and Jim knew that they knew that something was not right. He then looked over at his wife and sons, pausing again.

"Delay, reschedule. How long, when?"

"I do not know that, Mr. O'Francis."

"No." Then he paused for a good ten seconds. "I want to proceed. Julius, did you send in all the proper paperwork or what attorneys must do to prepare for a trial."

"Yes," came the response without hesitation.

"I see. Well, this is Reynolds County, notorious for its corruption. And we are fighting a corrupt political machine here which includes the clerk and, most likely, the judge. Fuck-it! The odds are against us! Let's do what we can! Swing away! Hope for a hit," Jim responded in total disgust. Julius looked at him momentarily, understood his metaphor, and rose.

"Your Honor, we will proceed with what we have," Julius informed the judge.

"Very well then, is the defense ready?" Judge Munis asked.

"We are your honor."

Jim mentally began to talk to himself. *It was, after all, Reynolds County. Anyone here knew it was the most political and corrupt county in the entire region. What sounded good and was the truth was not always how the legal system worked in Reynolds County. What more could I have expected? Take total control of your emotions. Do not break. Do not show any emotions. I have rolled the dice. I knew it was a big gamble from the very beginning. I knew the odds were against me. What the fuck did I think that some Irish fairy tale story would come out of all this? That is okay. I will give it my best shot. If I lose this fucking case, I will have justice in due time.*

At that point, calm appeared to come over him to all that had their eyes on Jim. He appeared as if he had been relieved of an overloaded burden. James Patrick smiled as he lowered his head to look at something on the table. Then he slowly looked up, took a deep breath, looked at his family, let the air out of his lungs, sat up straight in his chair, and thought, *Let's get this sham court case over with.*

Tim Harper turned out to be an unreliable witness. He did Jim no favors. His reluctance to elaborate on leading questions frustrated Julius. But, on the other hand, Jim knew him well and knew he would not place himself in the way of the political juggernaut in Reynolds County. Harper was all about

Harper. He was a coward. He had no honor—just another draft dodger from the Viet Nam era, which O'Francis had put aside during the years he had to work with him.

Tim Harper was excused after a lackluster and pathetic performance on the stand.

It was now 11:30 A.M., and Judge Munis called for a lunch break.

Jim would learn later from John O'Donovan, that Judge Munis, Curtis Feinstein, Damon Bales, Richard Finkel, and Jermaine Griffith all went to the restaurant across the street from the courthouse and shared a lengthy lunch together.

Dawn, Jim, and his sons met briefly at Julius's car. Tim Harper approached and began to talk about his testimony, and Julius sternly cut him off, stating in no uncertain terms,

"Mr. Harper, this case is not about you. It is about the damage that has been done to Mr. O'Francis! You did not do your "friend" and colleague justice while on the witness stand! Now, you can be excused. We are in an important conversation."

None of the O'Francis family spoke to Harper.

They all arrived back at the courthouse thirty minutes before the afternoon session began, and Julius and Jim talked over the line of questions he would give Teddy Hauler.

Julius stood and called his next witness, Mr. Teddy Hauler. Then, after all the facade of swearing to God was over, Julius began his line of questions.

He had been on the witness stand for over an hour and had not "struck out." Instead, Teddy had given a rock-solid testimony. The cross-examination did not rattle Teddy. Using Jim's every baseball term, Teddy got a hit every time a question was asked as he would freely elaborate on each question.

When Teddy was finally excused, Jim broke a small smile as he knew it struck a blow to the scum sitting across the room. He thought, *Your efforts to "K" Teddy failed. At the end of an inning! We scored runs. Even with Harper "striking out" each time.*

Jim knew he was behind in the "game" and feared that he would not have enough witnesses to counter the lies that would be told. And in the end, it was who won the game, not just an inning.

"I call Mary Jo Bankos as my next witness," Julius informed the court.

Again they went through all the buffalo dung, and Julius got down to business.

Julius took her through the morning of the incident at the corner gas station, which brought forth the now infamous letter. And Mary Jo answered and elaborated on each of his questions. She also testified that the people she had heard slander O'Francis were in the courtroom, and after Julius asked her to identify them, Mary Jo pointed to the defendants.

Curtis Feinstein failed in his efforts to trap Mary Jo in her testimony. He continued to change the method of questions, but none worked. Instead, he hammered at her, thinking she would break. Curtis' best effort in his cross-examination of Mary Jo was unsuccessful.

"Thank you, Mrs. Bankos. I have no further questions." Feinstein informed her, and the judge instructed her to step down from the witness chair.

Julius walked to the table where Jim sat. "Are you ready?"

"Well, since I am all that is left, I guess I had better be. So let's do our thing."

"Remember, Jim, relax. You know they will come after you."

Jim spent most of the afternoon on the witness stand, going through many questions and elaborating on them. Jim was hoping that the jury would understand why he had brought a lawsuit against Bales and Finkel for not only tainting his name but had cost him a means of providing for his family.

As Julius ended, Jim quickly said, "My father gave me this name without spot or blemish. I have passed my name to my sons without any blemish, and now it has been tainted because of many false allegations. What's in a name is not just words slung together. It is imperative to me as it was to my father and his father and to his father who arrived in this country in 1872 without any blemishes on the O'Francis name."

The cross-examination by Feinstein was harsh, and he did everything he could to trip Jim.

He came at him softly and then hard, redirecting several questions hoping that Jim would falter, but Jim did not. Instead, he remained very calm, and even as physically hot as it was in the courtroom, Jim didn't so much as break a bead of sweet on his brow, which, unlike Feinstein, had to wipe his forehead several times. Finally, as the five o'clock hour had passed, Feinstein finished his cross-examining of Jim, and the judge adjourned court for the day, leaving Feinstein to call his first witness at 9:00 A.M. on the second day of the trial.

Character Assassination

The following day, Jim was in an ill mood as he had gotten little sleep over the night. He did not feel good, and his little voice kept telling him to prepare for the worst. The ghosts of his past came in full force. The faces of his Asian enemies were Caucasian.

Julius seemed to be in a pleasant mood, and his father was in the same place he was the day before.

But there was no Holly present, something Jim was highly disappointed in, as he did not think Julius would have the same impact on Damon as Holly in the cross-examination. Finally, after all the buffalo chips were over, the judge asked if the defense was ready to call their first witness, and he informed the judge that he was.

"The defense calls Mrs. Janice Jones."

James P.'s eyes narrowed as Janice bounced into the courtroom and sat on the stand.

Ah, yes, their key witness, Jim thought. *The one person who supposedly had so much information concerning me that she is their major contributor to this case.*

Janice Jones, the mouthpiece for the Damon faction, has a significant pile of camel dung! Key witness, my ass! Hell, she is part of the whole damn conspiracy. She has been since I started in this damn corrupt fucking county! You, bitch, I could pop a cap on you here and now and sleep much better tonight!

After she swore to say nothing but the truth, Curtis Feinstein started his questions.

Janice being Janice rambled for an hour. Her fast type of speech was irritating. Her character assassination of Jim was expected, and Jim was not surprised. She did a masterful job. Her mendacity was spun like a delicate spider web. If one did not know the "black widow," you would most definitely have cause to believe Janice.

The cross-examination by Julius was relatively short, shorter than Jim would have liked. But he was not the attorney. What did he know? He was a simple teacher.

"Mrs. Jones, was Mr. O'Francis ever arrested for these alleged acts you have stated to the court?"

"No. But that…"

"Did the FBI ever contact you concerning these alleged acts?"

"No. But let me…"

"So you don't know for sure if Mr. O'Francis committed any of these acts of, as you have stated here today under oath and to this court, terrorism?"

"Well…"

Julius interrupted her. "Yes or no, Mrs. Jones."

"Well, ah, no, but…"

"Mrs. Jones," Julius continued before she could finish whatever she was going to say, "were you present during any of the alleged threats made by Mr. O'Francis to Mr. Finkel at the service station?"

"No."

"Have you seen the letter Mr. Bales wrote and sent to all the law enforcement agencies throughout the area?"

"No."

"Mrs. Jones, have you ever been present when Mr. O'Francis verbally threatened Mr. Bales or Mr. Finkel?"

"I have heard a lot of people…"

"Mrs. Jones, have you been present when Mr. O'Francis allegedly threatened Mr. Bales or Mr. Finkel? Answer yes or no." Julius's voice was stern and commanding as if he was agitated.

"Ahh, no."

"Mrs. Jones, have you ever seen Mr. O'Francis anywhere around your home, farm, or vehicle that you or your husband owns?"

"Well, no, but..."

Julius sharply cut her off. "So you cannot testify here on this day in this court of law that any of these alleged acts of terrorism that you claim took place was done by my client, Mr. James Patrick O'Francis?" Julius' voice was up another notch and even more stern as he pointed to Jim.

"Mr. ahh..." Janice did not know his last name.

Again with a sharp tone, Julius asked her to answer the question with a simple yes or no.

"NO." Janice was pissed. The tone of her answer gave her away. Her body language was evident as she had begun to move her shoulders as usual when verbalizing anger.

"Were you aware of any of the activities in Mr. Bales' office, or were you aware that Mr. Bales wrote or sent any letter concerning Mr. O'Francis to the School Board, law enforcement agencies, or judges surrounding this case?"

"Ahhh, NO." Again, her tone of voice was filled with anger. She was not allowed to continue verbally, which was her usual mode of operation.

"Mrs. Jones, has Mr. O'Francis ever personally threatened you?"

"Well, let me tell you..."

Again, Julius cut her off. "Answer the question Mrs. Jones with a simple yes or no."

"I would like to tell you...."

Julius interrupted her quickly. "Mrs. Jones, I asked you a question. Give me a yes or no answer."

Janice puffed up like a toad and sat silent.

"Your Honor, please instruct the witness to answer the question."

"Mrs. Jones, you have to answer the question." His voice was not a stern judge but a more polite, "Would you please?" tone. One that Jim took note of instantly. It appeared to Jim that the judge was reluctant to instruct Janice to answer the question. However, Jim had already resigned himself to the fact that the judge was impartial in the case. The finite details Jim would learn later.

"I would like to, but he won't let me."

Jim was not at all surprised at her comment to the judge.

At that point, Julius stated, "Your Honor."

In what appeared to be a friendly tone, Judge Munis instructed Janice to answer the questions as presented with a yes or no.

Feinstein rose at that point and stated that Julius was harassing his witness. To Jim's surprise, Judge Munis dismissed the objection.

"Now, Mrs. Jones, let me ask you again. Did Mr. O'Francis ever threaten you at any time when you and he worked in the same school?"

"NO!"

Julius turned to the judge. "Your honor, I have no further questions for this witness. However, I do reserve the right to recall her."

"You may step down, Mrs. Jones," Judge Munis stated.

Feinstein quickly rose from his seat. "Your Honor, the defense calls Mr. Stan MacNolin to the stand."

After all the "I swear to God crap," who he was, who he worked for, and where he lived was through, Feinstein started his questions.

MacNolin did his best to paint Jim O'Francis as a person who would harm Finkel and Bales. He used the horse barn story as he knew Jim's love of horses. Stating that Jim had related his dislike for Mr. Bales to him while grooming several of his horses. Stan testified that Jim had indicated that Richard Finkel and Ms. Alcott were in an inmate relationship.

MacNolin went through all the dislikes of Jim's coaching and teaching, more of the same type of character assassination Jones had uttered from her mendacious mouth. Julius had to object on several occasions concerning his classroom, as Stan was repeating what someone allegedly told him.

Curtis Feinstein started to his table and turned.

"I have one more question. Mr. MacNolin, have you and Mr. Harper discussed Mr. O'Francis' coaching?"

"Yes."

"Would you tell the court about what was discussed?"

"Well, Mr. Harper told me that he was disappointed in his conduct and was becoming an embarrassment to him and the school. So he had to talk to him about how he acted."

"Did Mr. Harper ever tell you that he had to report this conduct to the principal or the athletic director?"

"Yes."

"No further questions at this time, your Honor."

Julius turned to Jim and asked, "Are you aware of this?"

"Some." He replied.

Judge Dan Munis looked at Julius. "Do you wish to cross-examine Mr. MacNolin?"

"Yes, your Honor. One moment please."

"Some, what does that mean?" Julius asked O'Francis.

"It simply means that the only thing in the entire testimony that had any truth in it, to my knowledge, was that I did go to the horse barn, just as I have stated in my testimony to Feinstein. As to anything else, I do not know whatsoever. And I repeat myself here, Julius, I did not have any conversation concerning Maura Alcott with Stan at the barn or elsewhere. Julius that did not happen. Fact!"

Julius rose slowly but stayed at the table beside Jim. Before Julius could speak, Jim's voice became harsh, stating he did not know of Harper's alleged statements. So, therefore, I say to you, Julius, that Tim Harper never, and I mean never ever, had a conversation with me over any inappropriate conduct because there was none! That, Mr. Donatello, is a fact!" As Jim O'Francis rose to become eye level. Jim's eyes told Julius Donatello everything.

"Mr. MacNolin, do you like Mr. O'Francis?"

"Well, I don't know."

"Well, either you do or don't, which is it?"

"Well, I guess I would say I don't."

"How often did you talk to Mr. O'Francis?"

"Very little."

"So, you could say you do not know him well?"

"Ahhh, well, no, I don't guess so."

"Did you attend all your son's home games?"

"Yes, and several that were away."

"Have you ever seen Coach O'Francis thrown out of a game?"

"I don't think so."

"You don't think so. Either you have or you have not. Which is it, Mr. MacNolin?"

"Ah, I have not."

"Have you ever seen him in an angry confrontation with an umpire?"

"Ahh, I don't believe I have."

"You don't think so? Either you have, Mr. McNolin, or you have not. Which is it?"

"Well, I would have to say no."

"Have you ever seen or been present when Coach Harper had to confront Coach O'Francis about anything he may or may not have done during a game or at any practices?"

There was a rather long pause as if Stan was thinking.

Julius did not let it linger. "Your answer, please, Mr. MacNolin."

"Ahhh, no, I don't believe I have."

"Mr. MacNolin, have you seen Mr. Bales and Mr. Finkel's letter concerning Mr. O'Francis?"

"No."

"Did your son ever tell you that he did not like Coach O'Francis?"

"Ahhh, no."

"Did he ever complain about him as a teacher?"

"No."

"What kind of grades did he make under Mr. O'Francis?"

"Good ones."

"What does that mean, good ones? Give me a letter grade so the jury can understand what you mean by good ones."

"He made A's and B's in his class."

"So you can testify today that you had no complaints concerning Mr. O'Francis teaching your son?"

"Well, not really. But I heard..."

"Thank you. I have no more questions for the witness at this time."

Judge Munis excused MacNolin from the stand.

After going through both Bales' mentally deranged skewed testimony and Finkel's rendition of a fictional horror story, which took up the rest of the day, the trial was done. All that remained was closing by both attorneys.

Julius' cross-examination of both was done reasonably well but not as well as Holly Donatello's would have been. Julius did not have the skills to bring the very worst out of Damon or, for that matter, Finkel. She was a very skilled attorney and could set one up with her questions and have you tell the lies they thought to be the truth, revealing the person they were. However, there was nothing James P. could do about her absence. He just had to go with what cards he had in his hand and hope that Julius could win the game with his closing statement.

Judges and Jurors

The judges had done their jobs. They had communicated with each other, as they had done in other cases, and the clerk of the Reynolds County Court rewarded them with a tiny bit of graft. But, of course, the amount was nothing compared to the more significant cases he had done for both judges depending on who was sitting on the Circuit Court. Nevertheless, a little cash in the pocket never bothered either the judges or Jermaine, who got a moderate fee for making sure that some verdicts went the way of the cash flow.

Judge Daniel MacMuller had been deep in the pockets of the heavy hammers of the political party of Reynolds County. However, he had been well cared for by a few more significant and influential companies within the county. The counties surrounding Reynolds also had a few large companies that paid a nice fee for services to the judge when cases came before him. So, taking graft for making the law work for whoever could afford the cost of "blind justice" had slowly become a source of substantial income.

Judge Dan Munis had his closet of secrets. His drug and prostitute habit grew yearly, and his lucrative salary for sitting on the bench was strained to the max. Nevertheless, the extra payments for favorites passed on in the name of "blind justice," large or small, were all welcomed.

The jury had been given instructions from the judge, of which Jim was savvy enough to have caught the intent of his instructions and knew that his case was in the "shitter." But, depending on whether or not there were any honest people on the jury, that was very unlikely.

As Judge Munis finished his little "according to the law" instructions, he looked at Jim, who had locked his eyes on the judge. Then, Dan Munis paused in speech and movement momentarily as O'Francis's cold, hard look caught his attention. At that moment, Jim knew that he knew.

But Jim also knew that he had the power, and that was all that mattered, no matter how small and insignificant his case may be. Judge Munis' pompous attitude quickly returned as he instructed the jurors to retire to the jury room.

The five jurors rose and strolled to a conference room beside the judge's office. O'Francis took a deep breath and looked over at his family. He scanned the room and saw that Holly had arrived after all was over. There was no consolation for Jim, who was in no mood for her conversation; for that matter, outside of his family, he did not care to talk to anyone. For all his earlier beliefs in Holly and her family of attorneys, he felt betrayed by the lack of interest in his simple civil suit. Instead, he felt that they used him to get the firm's newest member some experience other than court-appointed cases.

Jim wandered off briefly to gather his thoughts and mentally prepare himself for the outcome his little voice told him it would be. *It is human nature for people to be corruptible,* he thought. His little voice continued talking to him, telling him everything about the trial had been corrupted. It would not have made any difference if he had an F. Lee Bailey as his attorney. The die had been cast. This was Reynolds County which had earned its reputation long before his little case had made its way to the courtroom. Clerks, attorneys, and judges were tainted, and James Patrick O'Francis' belief in honor and integrity in the judicial system was as dissipating as a fart in the wind.

Inside the jury room, a problem seemed to have arisen. All the jurors did not adhere to what the judge had instructed them to consider. The letter was written and sent, so for two jurors, that was enough to cast their vote for Jim. The other three insisted that the judge instructed them to consider that O'Francis still had his teaching job and that he had not lost any significant money from his family income.

Jermaine, now in the judge's chambers, stated that he felt it had gone well and that the verdict would come quickly. Then he and Judge Munis laughed.

Inside the jury room, the conversation continued.

"Look, the principal, what's his name?" Harold asked.

"Damon Bales," Tamura replied.

"What he did was out and out wrong. Hell, I sure would not like someone to write a letter to all the police forces and tell them I was a terrorist. Look, people, in this day and time, police take that kind of stuff seriously."

"I think he brought it on himself," Tamura stated.

"How?"

"Well, according to the testimony of that Jones woman..."

Pauline cut her off. "You know people; you may believe her if you want. But for me, I think she lied through her teeth! Just something about her. I didn't believe a word she said. So my vote stays the same. Also, how did she get involved in this case anyway? I mean, wasn't the case about the letter? All she did was lambast Mr. O'Francis, right?"

"I have to agree with Pauline," Harold said. "I think several people lied for Bales. And another thing, isn't lying under oath some crime? I mean, you take an oath to tell the truth on the witness stand, right? I think I heard that somewhere."

Several moments passed, and no one commented on the lying aspect of the question.

"I don't think Mr. O'Francis was damaged all that much from just a single letter. I mean, he still has his job. Right?" Randall stated.

Jim paced back and forth from outside the building to the long corridor past the offices and the courtroom.

The entire Donatello legal counsel was now present in the corridor. Jim had a meaningless conversation with all three for a few minutes. He then walked outside and got some fresh air.

He was still running the whole ordeal over in his mind with every word the witnesses said. He was good at remembering what people said. The way Julius handled the case. Holly could not be present when they put Damon on the stand. The entire trial began to smell like a three-day-old dead fish.

He rested his hands on the gray-painted rail connecting the building and led some ten feet toward the parking lot. Stepping back several steps, leaving his hands on the rail, Jim stretched his back. Several upper disks popped as he arched his body down between his arms. His little voice told him that the day would not end well for him. He should be mentally prepared for the worst.

Fuck! I do not like the way Julius handled the entire frigging thing! What the fuck! His first real case, or was it that I would not settle with what the sons-of-bitches were offering me to settle out of court?

Then he began to speak aloud very softly to himself.

"I do not give a royal rat's ass what they think. However, I know that Julius damn sure did not do all he could have done.

I wonder just why all my witnesses were left off the list! I mean, come on here. Would not a good attorney have all that shit checked and double-checked?

It was good that no one was present, or they would have thought Jim had lost his mind because he was talking to someone not present.

He walked his feet forward, standing erect. He looked out over the backside of the town and the business and government buildings with people coming and going, all with their own problems. He turned sharply to his right. He returned to the building to put on his best political face, telling himself to choose his words carefully. He tried staying close to his wife and sons. That way, he was less likely to speak ill of his counsel or any member of the counsel's family.

Jermaine had left for a good 45 minutes and returned to the judge's office.

"What the hell. I know it doesn't take that long to find in favor of Defense. Hell-O, Dan, did they not get what you were telling them? This was to be a done deal. Who did we miss?"

"The "we" part is, I don't know. The question is, who did you miss? There is no "we" in that," as Judge Munis curtly corrected the clerk of the court.

"Well, you know what I mean."

"I will admit this is taking a little longer than I expected," Munis confessed.

"Hell, people! This is a simple civil case, not a murder trial. What's the problem? Look, I want to go home. It's late, and we have already gone over this too many times," Kermit stated in a firm voice.

"I really don't care. I think the letter is damaging!" Pauline insisted.

"Look, Pauline," Randall stated, trying to plead with her to vote in favor of the Defense so they could get out and go home.

"O'Francis is not out of anything. He has not lost his job, I mean, as I have stated several times now, as has Kermit. He still has his teaching job. If he lost his job, I would be all for you. But there is no real damage done. Right?"

Harold left most of the talking to everyone else in the room. Pauline was doing his talking, and he felt she was right, so he felt no need to repeat the same thing she was stating.

"So Harold, you have not said anything in a long while. What do you say? You are voting with the rest of us, right?" Tamura asked.

"I keep thinking about what he said while on the stand."

"He who?" Tamura stated in an agitated voice.

"O'Francis."

"Okay, so what?" Kermit said.

"He stated that a name is special, that our name is special. That to tarnish that name is damaging. I know it's not his exact words, but something like that. Oh yeah, what was that about his father passing it on to him, and he wanted to pass it on to his sons? Oh yeah, and with a clean slate."

"So, what's your point?" Tamura stated, her voice displaying her dislike for the long debate.

The room fell silent for several minutes.

"Okay, Tamura, I don't think you will ever understand his point. But you know, I do. But for the sake of dragging this out any longer..."

It had been three hours since the jury had been deliberating. Jim had just returned from another walk outside and had sat by his sons and wife when Officer Kuntz came out into the hallway and announced that the jury was returning. Last scene of a five-year play, one that James Patrick had not liked and would not likely ever be in the presence of again.

Jim was standing at parade rest alongside Julius. Judge Dan Munis asked, "Has the jury reached a verdict?"

"We have your Honor."

"You may read the verdict."

"We, the jury, find in favor of the Defense."

Jim never moved. The gang of jackals celebrated with their friends and witnesses.

His little voice had tried to prepare him, yet he was crushed inside. His outer demeanor was professional, never expressing any emotion.

The clerk rushed to the judge, handed him a piece of paper, and spoke with him for a moment. Judge Munis looked over toward Julius and Jim and then requested Julius to approach.

Jim was still standing at parade rest, motionless. Then, finally, he slowly turned his head toward his family, and their faces told how they felt. Then, eventually, his eyes shifted to the back of the courtroom. "The Man" and O'Donovan were standing separated on the long benches in the courtroom, one at the far end next to the wall and the other at the entrance to the courtroom, both looking toward Jim, neither showing as if either knew him.

Julius returned to the table. "We need to talk in a room in the back." Julius requested that his father join them, making their way to a conference room.

After they sat, Julius asked, "Jim did you discuss Richard Finkel's alleged affair openly in your classroom?"

"No. I answered that question on the stand. Why?"

"Because the clerk presented this letter to the judge."

He handed the letter to Jim to read. He quickly read it. A student who had never been in any of his classes signed it. Jenny Bosworth claimed that Jim had talked to his History class about Finkel and Maura Alcott.

Jim exploded, abruptly standing and scooting his chair back with his legs. He held the letter up toward Julius and Lucius and stated loudly, "This is a god-damn lie!"

"All that may be true, but you will be investigated for perjury by the commonwealth attorney."

"I am going to be investigated for PERJURY? Is this some god-damn sick joke?"

"Not so loud, Jim. Someone will hear you. The judge is in the next room."

"Ohh, wow, the judge will hear me...Well, Julius, I really do not give two fucks at this point! Go tell the "good" judge to come in here, and I will state the same to his corrupt fucking face!"

Julius and Lucius just looked at one another.

Jim tossed the letter toward Julius. It slid to him on the shiny, highly polished table.

"Another thing Julius!" His voice instantly turned to a very calm and deadly cold tone.

"Jenny Bosworth was never in my class. The school records can confirm that! So how did she hear me discuss anything she claimed in her letter concerning Finkel?"

"Well, I don't know that Jim. All I know is that the clerk informed the judge that you had committed perjury during your testimony."

"The clerk told the judge? Now I am not in a perfect frame of mind at present...But how in the hell would the CLERK know if I had or had not committed perjury? I mean, can you tell me that!"

"No, Jim, I cannot."

"Well, Mr. Lucius Donatello, you are the experienced one here. The head of your law firm. Can you tell me?"

"No, Mr. O'Francis, I cannot."

"Well, I am telling YOU AND YOU," O'Francis indicated with a nod to both the Donatello attorneys. "That I did not commit perjury! FACT! Now, if anyone in this GREAT judicial system wants to find the REAL truth and who committed perjury, then they only need to look as far as Bales, Finkel, and their witnesses! BUT, hey, we all know that that just ain't going to happen! So let me tell you two something, let them investigate me. Hell, it will not be the first time I have been investigated. I have been cleared each time. Do you know why? Because I tell the truth. That, gentlemen, is the real problem in this great judicial system. The one you, Julius, claim is the best in the world!"

Then there was a rather long pause.

"Let me end this little meeting by stating I will never make this mistake again! Never!"

Just as Jim began to turn, the elder of the Donatello legal minds spoke. "Mr. O'Francis, may I ask what you mean?"

"What I mean what?"

"With the statement, you will never make this mistake again."

Jim did a complete military about-face, took several steps around the corner of the table, looked directly at the two attorneys, and in a shallow unemotional voice, stated, "It is quite simple, Mr. Donatello. I will be the legal system. I will receive rightful justice. Your system is corrupted. I may not be some great legal mind, but even this simple teacher can see through this."

In a quick defense of the great legal system the United States has in place, Julius spoke. "It is better than anyplace else in the world, Mr. O'Francis."

"That Mr. Julius Donatello is very debatable! Sir!"

James Patrick left the two attorneys that day, hoping he would only have to meet one more time to discuss if he wanted to appeal the verdict in his case, which he could not afford. In addition, he knew the outcome would be the same. The judicial system was corrupt!

The Commonwealth Attorney investigated James Patrick for his alleged perjury. After a month of investigation, the Commonwealth Attorney, Anita Lindamood, found the letter was a false statement. After investigating the allegations, Ms. Lindamood found that the Bosworth girl was never in James O'Francis' classes, just as he had stated. Thus, as a result, the finding for perjury was that James O'Francis was not guilty, and a case against him was never brought. Jim had told the truth. The case was closed. But the truth did not matter.

THE INSANITY OF WAR

O'Francis's mind could not let the day's events go, and his night was filled with the events of anger and violence. His psychologist had told him that anger, fear, and guilt resulted from his nightmares.

Jim did not always agree with what his mental doctor had to say, although she was a renowned expert in her field.

His reaction to the death of Rusty still, after so many years, haunted his nights. And out of all the horrors of Viet Nam he had experienced, the one that seemed to reoccur more often was his closest friend's death. Although his nightmares had not occurred as frequently over the past several years, his analysis was because he had not been under any work-related stress.

He still had no clue as to what triggered his nightmares. It did not make sense to O'Francis. If nightmares were triggered because of anger, fear, or guilt, how could one explain away the fact that there were times when he would have a good day filled with happiness with lots of smiles and laughter, joy and love, always coming home to a wife that he adored and knew she loved and supported him.

Yet, in the middle of what had started as a peaceful night's sleep, he would experience Viet Nam's sights, sounds, and smells. Suddenly he would find himself on the floor beside his bed in the prone position in a cold sweat, breathing heavily, looking across a dark room for something that was not there.

Another simple mission was to recon an area that did not need to be reconned, so O'Francis thought.

Hell, everyone knew who and what was there. But someone, some arrogant brass ass bastard, needed the information. The "Spooks," the good ole military intelligence, SOG, CIA ran the operation. They required this critical information. *Pure bullshit,* O'Francis thought as he readied himself for a three-day trek through the fuckin' jungle, which often more than not turned out to be more than three days.

He had been in an ill mood for over a month. He had no one to talk to, so he bottled everything up inside. He spoke to no one and did his job with reckless disregard for his life.

The orders were to "nab" a high-ranking VC, or even better, a North Vietnamese Regular, preferably an officer. Captain Thompson's last words to O'Francis were to not take any unnecessary chances. Thompson felt that the mission was not all that important. But he, too, was following orders.

"Just get what you can and get the hell out of the valley. It is not a good place to be, as the activity was heavy, and everyone knows it."

Two Americans, one Special Forces Staff Sergeant named Michael Grimes from Georgia and one Ranger, along with four well-trained "Yard's," left the compound on a mission of doom for O'Francis.

It was near nightfall when the "Star-light" patrol lifted off from the camp, a very short flight, and by darkness, they were in position for their first night under a star-filled sky, if one could see the little twinkles in the sky from the depth of a heavy jungle canopy. O'Francis had gotten to the point that everything bothered him. The bugs, which had not bothered him before, or so he had thought, seemed just to irritate him more than ever. Sounds, any sound bothered him. First, he would snap at the "Yards" when they asked him for guidance. Then he would apologize moments later realizing what he had done. He knew they had lost much more than he had, yet he could not let it go. As he lay silent on the jungle floor, the anger built inside. He got little sleep when he was in camp and on patrol, he could not rest at all. His mind would not shut down. Most could not rest on patrol, but specially trained personnel learned how to get a little sleep or relax their eyes and mind when and where they could.

Daylight came and they were up and moving like some camouflaged jungle cat searching out their prey. One enemy patrol passed after another, unknowing that they were being watched, all wearing black, hauling their supplies from one point to another. Deeper and deeper, the "Star-light" patrol went into the mouth of the valley of doom.

It was genuinely insane what they were doing, but *"it was vitally important"* to get a live North Vietnamese Regular. Another "VC" patrol passed within a few feet of him. O'Francis thought, *Like the son of bitch is going to tell "whomever" anything.*

And snaring an NVR is like fucking zero. What the fuck were these dumb-asses thinking?"

Grimes was not at all happy about the mission himself. He was a veteran Special Forces Sergeant on his third tour. He knew how O'Francis felt about it, but they were good soldiers and did what they were told. The odds were that IF they could nab one, they would because they were good at playing the game of guerrilla warfare, as good if not better than the very people they played against. SOG wouldn't get "jack shit" out of him.

Day two and day three were repeats of day one. No Regulars. If none decided to stroll by, they would have to settle for a simple VC, something they knew they could get in places a hell of a lot safer. Not that they ever went anywhere safe, but there were worse places to be caught in a firefight than others, and a lot easier to capture a simple VC.

Now getting a Regular and an officer to boot, one must go where the "big dogs" ran. The next big problem was picking a very small patrol which was not all that easy. And from where they were, getting out after a firefight, even a small one, did not have the best of odds, something Jim was sure the odd makers would not place their money down on.

It was very late in the afternoon. O'Francis had just looked at his watch, 1715 hours, when movement was spotted. Again they prepared for the snatch as the sound of a VC patrol approached. As "luck" would have it, if one would like to consider having a ten-man Viet Cong patrol with three North Vietnamese Officers in the very middle of the patrol, "luck," then the "Star-light" patrol was the luckiest bunch of guerrilla fighters that ever rolled the dice.

O'Francis' eyes got big. His heart pounded heavily when he saw the three tan uniforms trimmed in red stroll by. The "Cong" wore sandals. The NVR wore boots.

Everyone, down to the last man, knew just what to do. The trap, so to speak, was sprung—a very short firefight with the leaves popping from the returning fire of the VC patrol. Then, the whizzing of near misses as Jim switched to another magazine.

The "Star-light" patrol had no wounded or KIA's, which did not always happen. The element of surprise and experience gave Jim and the company the advantage. But now, they had three North

Vietnamese Regulars officially as POWs. One was wounded in his right upper thigh and lower left abdomen.

The other two would have some facial bruising and maybe a fractured jaw from the butt of a rifle. Other than that, unharmed. Two sandal-pounding VC were also captured. Jim knew they were not needed, and O'Francis was in no mood for any of their mouths. Nor was he about to drag five POWs through an enemy-infested jungle just so some starched fatigued high ranking, numb-nutted, pencil dicked officer could interrogate them and get squat.

Without warning, he drew his .45 from his shoulder holster, walked up to the two VC, popped a cap on each "dead" center of the forehead, and replaced his pistol in his black shoulder holster. He reached his right hand to his upper left shoulder and removed his knife from the black leather sheath, placing the blade against the side of the dead VC's right head, slicing the right ear off like a surgeon with a scalpel. He repeated the same to the second one and replaced the knife in the sheath, then he turned and walked ten feet toward the wounded North Vietnamese Regular officer.

Grimes quickly moved to his side and, in a low voice, asked, "O'Francis, what the fuck are you doing? For Christ's sakes, man."

O'Francis' eyes told him everything. There was nothing there—an abyss of darkness.

He turned to face Timothy M. Grimes, and in a shallow voice that had no feeling in it, he answered,

"This is personal! It's for Rusty. We will have two to haul back, for who the fuck ever!"

As the two stood three feet away from the NVA officer, he spoke, "Ban lâ Nguoi lay-tai" (*You are the ear taker*.) The officer said in Vietnamese in a painful voice.

Jim slowly turned his head to look down at the officer. He slowly removed his pistol from the holster and slowly cocked the hammer back. Jim dropped his arm to his side. He looked directly into the eyes of the NVA officer. "Phen. Ai em Nguoi lay-tai." (*Yes. I am the ear taker*.) He had learned enough Vietnamese to understand some of their languages and speak some.

Grimes stood beside O'Francis but did not respond. Tim had been where Jim was, and once again, the two locked eyes. Timothy Grimes saw nothing but a deep black void. He then turned and moved along the trail some fifty feet to help secure the two other North Vietnamese Regulars' hands behind their backs. The "Yards" and Grimes started on their escape route. Again, O'Francis looked into the officer's eyes. He raised his arm from 36 inches away, extending it straight down toward the officer's head, and popped the cap, leaving the man limp with just his leg muscles twitching.

O'Francis felt nothing as he slowly replaced his pistol in the holster. He then removed his knife and took the North Vietnamese Captain's right and left ear, placing them in his left fatigue pocket with the other two. He stood for a moment; silence filled the air, not so much as a sound, not even a breeze. He stood looking at the three soldiers. It was as if he was not where he was, as if he was removed from all the insanity that had engulfed him for the past few months.

"Damn this place!" He then turned and rejoined his patrol in moments, hoping to make the PZ without meeting any of their guerrilla counterparts.

Jim awoke sweating, and then he shook his entire upper body as if the temperature was in the teens. His heart was beating overtime. Then, looking around the dark bedroom, orienting himself, he quietly got out of the bed where Dawn was soundly sleeping and went to the living room, where he spent the next two hours pondering and talking with his spirit guide.

Several months passed, and the short walks in the forest were not helping James Patrick. He liked walking in the winter forest, especially in the snow. Jim's Irish setter was always just a few yards to his front or either side. Darby would stop when Jim would stop and come to be at his side. The cold winds turned Jim's face red, and the stinging tingling followed. But, on the other hand, he loved the pure silence of it all. Just the wind was all one could hear.

The early spring arrived as the trees put on their new green clothes. Jim would take long walks, observing the small animals and a deer on a rare occasion.

However, that was not helping his mental state. He would have to return home to face yet another day of work. He knew he had to get away for a long while. He had to go somewhere he could think, somewhere he felt safe, somewhere he could breathe, and to feel the earth under him at night, where he could smell the forest floor of decayed leaves and deep dark soil on his clothes, hands, face, and arms. Jim adored Dawn, and as much as he always looked forward to coming home to her, be it from his work or his forest retreat, he needed someplace he did not have to return home daily and wash off the forest smell. Or the stench from some student's fucked up house. Jim placed all the blame on the condition of such homes on the sorry-ass, good-for-nothing leeching parents of society. Jim had a lot of empathy for his students who lived in the squalor of such type homes.

Once again, his mind was not where it should be. He was as unbalanced as when fate connected him to his "Twin Flame" many years in the past. Then, she pierced his darkness and brought balance to his life.

He desperately needed time away, night and day spent alone with just the forest. Jim's "twin flame" knew her "twin flame" was in deep pain, and there was nothing she could do. Dawn knew he would not talk about it, and she never inquired. Instead, she tried to understand her husband's mood swings—his often long-distance looks and absence of responses when she would talk to him or ask a question.

SUICIDE

Jim was struggling mentally and lacking sleep. In addition, his ghosts were making frequent visits, leaving Jim more depressed.

It was a typical evening for Dawn and Jim: favorite television shows and a little conversation. Jim looked over at his adoring "Twin-Flame."

"Dawn, I think I will check out of the hotel."

A moment of pause. She calmly stated without emotion or looking at Jim.

"Well, don't do it here in the house. Go up on the flat and do it."

Nothing else was said.

By the week's end of dealing with the school system's ignorance, stupidity, and insanity and the cult following teachers to the oligarchical madman principal, Damon Bales, Jim's mental state had reached its breaking point, and the weight had become too much to carry. He could not think logically, which kept him semi-balanced. He had too many demons playing in his mind, all triggered by the totalitarian principal he was currently working for. Jim picked up his .45 military pistol and, without saying a word, walked the one-hundred yards up the sloping topography to the area he and Dawn had dubbed "the flat," an area of their land measuring 100x30x40 feet. Jim had built a large fire pit where they could enjoy evenings and nights together by a glowing fire. Jim took no chair with him to the flat. Years earlier, he had split a large tree some eight feet long and had made a bench log for sitting.

His mind was flashing one image after another. Events in his life that had altered his whole perspective—the loss of his daughter Christine in the first year of his marriage, then came the three A.M. knock on his front door as the State Troopers informed him and Dawn of the shocking loss of their thirty-year-old son in a fiery head-on collision with a tracker and trailer, the horrifying events in Viet Nam, and the just and unjust actions he had done out of vengeance for losing his best friend, witnessing the horror of the atrocities by the VC on their own people. As he sat on the hand-hued oak log, the flashes sped up one picture after another—the mistake he had made by moving his family to the mountains he loved. His dream location had been the upper Shenandoah Valley region. But would that have been different? He would never know.

His thumb pulled the trigger back on the 1911 .45 caliber pistol. He paused momentarily, and then he verbally stated.... "Fuck-it!" Jim put the pistol up into the roof of his mouth. His thumb released the safety on the side of the pistol. He began to squeeze the trigger slowly. It only takes five pounds of pressure to release the trigger, sending the firing pin into the cap and firing the bullet out of the barrel, sending it through the top of his head, ending his life. The trigger began to move ever so slightly. Then a loud, clear voice called his name. "Jim, stop!" He let up on the trigger. He looked to his left and his right. He slowly lowered the pistol from his mouth. Jim rested his hand and pistol on his right knee. He again looked all around the flat. It was the voice he had heard since he was a teen. However, this time he knew he had heard her voice as if she was present in real-time. Jim stood. Her voice again was clear and pronounced as she continued. "You are not done with your mission."

He sat back down on his log bench, his elbows on his knee. The pistol in his right hand was hanging in between his knees. With tears running down his cheeks, he mentally responded to his spirit guide. "Fine! What mission?" And again, she repeated. "You are not done yet. Complete your mission. Adjust and overcome. Time is endless. Fate."

After several hours of silent meditation and several bouts of tears, he walked back to his home and to the woman he adored. That night as Jim lay beside his beloved Dawn and closed his eyes, a song began to play in his mind.

"I've just closed my eyes again; climbed aboard the dream weaver train…take away my worries of today…
…And leave tomorrow behind…Ooh, dream weaver, I believe you can get me through the night…
…Ooh, dream weaver, I believe we can reach the morning light…."

Retreat

It was late July, and Jim had gone to the mountains again to recover. He could not shake the loss of the trial that had all the signs of political corruption. He was very bitter over how his attorney had handled the entire case. Poorly and incompetent would be a light verbal tongue-lashing.

Hate was eating him alive. It had been the visits to Viet Nam that hatred had made him wary to the perils of his teaching job. He knew these feelings very well, but he was not in Vietnam. He was in the good ole U.S. of A. So he could not do what he did then.

Jim had moved from one campsite to another for days, finding a spot he liked and felt secure to camp for a night. Then, when the sun rose, he was up and broke camp, walking through the mountain forest with stealth, observing the wildlife and enjoying the peacefulness of Nature.

Often a deer would stop suddenly and look at the strange figure twenty-five yards away. They would smell the air, turn one ear and another, using all their senses to try and detect what it was that was not normal to the area they traveled, a stare down between homosapien and deer. Jim would never move when these events would occur, often remaining motionless for as long as five to eight minutes.

The deer would then flick their tails a few times and stroll off and disappear into the thickness of the forest.

Most of the wildlife was small and paid little attention to O'Francis as they went about their daily survival routine. Something Jim was trying extremely hard to do. His mental game had to be put back on track, and he had to adapt and overcome his present adversities and move on with his life.

Jim had been walking the strip job for miles, the ever continuous or what would seem, one to two hundred yards wide path, cut off the near tops of mountains to extract the rich mineral called coal. A snake-like lush green carpet of grazing area, restored by the mine owners, ordered by the federal government, which had, in essence, turned into a positive environmental project. But he never made camp on the "stripped" land. Instead, he would calculate his daylight and make sure he found a break in the "high wall" to go to the top of a ridge or part of a mountain top. He never went down off the "strip job" to find a campsite.

Usually, in the early morning hours, he could catch the wildlife as they, too, stirred from a night of rest. His "field glasses," as he often referred to them, most people just called them binoculars, were used frequently during his trip, not just to observe the wildlife but to make sure he did not come upon any humans.

He had paused for a rest and some map and compass readings as he decided to follow the ridgeline for the morning instead of the more effortless traveling on the ribbon of tall grasses with the few saplings that dotted the old "strip job" below him. He had never seen a bear in all the times he had been in the area's forest.

As he sat on the top of a peaked point and major out-cropping before the topography dropped sharply down to a natural break in the ridge, with a breeze blowing through the trees below him, he heard an abnormal amount of noise being created. His "topo" map indicated a brook leading down the mountain's south side. He carefully scanned the thick underbrush with field glasses in hand, seeking any small open areas between the trees where he could see what was making all the noise.

Then he saw movement, a black bear with two cubs working their way up the hill directly toward him. He waited and watched as the cubs played and the mother looked for food. Then, finally, she took her cubs around the north side of the ridge some fifty yards from where Jim sat. For the moments he had watched these magnificent creatures, his mind had been free, at peace. He was relaxed and felt at ease. Calm had come over him.

He was on his fourth day, and according to his map, there was a road about three miles in the westerly direction he was traveling. It led off the mountain, most likely an old logging road, maybe a "strip mining" road, or a gas well road, as the area was dotted with gas wells.

He took his time going up and down the hump-backed ridge, as he did not want to return to "civilization." He was very much at ease by himself in the arms of Mother Nature.

His mind often went to Dawn and what she was doing or what she would do if something happened to him. His adoration for her was immeasurable. But he knew he needed to get his "shit" together and get back home and do what needed to be done that made her house a home.

It took Jim the better part of the morning to trek the three miles he had set for himself, arriving at the top of a bluff overlooking the road leading out onto the flat grasses of the "stripped" land. He was soaked from sweat, and a light breeze swept across the top of the ridge. He removed his backpack, and then he stripped to his waist, draping his gray tee shirt on one bush, his "jungle" fatigue top on another to dry. He preferred the old fatigues he had used in his youth to the modern-day type of fatigues. He searched for several years before he found the Vietnam era fatigues and wore them each time he escaped into his forest world. His leather shoulder holster was just as wet, which he hung on yet another bush branch. He removed his boots and socks and then pulled a gun cleaning kit from his pack, wiping down his .357 but not removing the quarter-ounce shot in the cylinder.

His line of sight to the stripped field below was reasonably good. Placing his field glasses to his eyes, he scanned the view area and spotted two does grazing at the edge of the field. He observed the deer with his natural sight, and he ate another pack of dehydrated food and two granola bars. His water was now running low, but he knew he would be home by nightfall. He could not stand to be without water. He had gone through that once in his life and knew the value of the precious liquid.

His plan to descend the mountain would lead him to Emmanuel's farm. Then, he would call Dawn to come get him.

He had been resting for two hours, writing in his journal, laying back on the ground, watching the clouds passing overhead, absorbing the sounds of nature, and dozing off to a light nap. Then, the crows in the area began to sound "breaking news." Then, Jim's ears caught the sound of something not natural to nature, a human machine, a motorized vehicle approaching in the distance. It seemed odd to Jim, with his hearing as bad as it was, but when he was alone in the forest, he could pick up sounds one hundred percent better, more prominent, at a farther distance.

He rose quickly, gathered his not yet dry clothes, strapped on his holster, shoved his gun in its place, put his socks and boots on in a hurry, slung his backpack on, and worked his way some fifty yards down the bluff where he could observe the approaching vehicle. As he settled into the thick undergrowth, his thoughts went to the sounds of the crows...*Nature at its best, and crows, "the news reporters" of nature.*

In minutes, a sports utility vehicle stopped at a rusty-chained gate. Jim watched with his field glasses. A man on the passenger side got out with heavy-duty bolt cutters and cut the chain, swinging the gate open and allowing the Chevrolet Blazer to enter the flat. They drove directly toward Jim, coming to a stop a quarter of a mile from the entrance in a concave area of the high wall, out of view of the gate area.

Jim sat high above the two men, looking almost straight at them. Using his field glasses from his concealed vantage point, he could see directly into the Blazer.

Ten minutes passed, then the two got out and looking around the area, both men relieved themselves of a full bladder, one looking directly up at Jim's observation point.

In O'Francis' camouflaged position, he looked directly into the whites of the man's eyes. For O'Francis, he was in his element, cloaked and observing his "enemy." So many times, he had been in the same position he was now. His veins felt hot with the unexpected rush of adrenaline.

Like a bolt of lightning, he was in the jungles of Eastern Laos, looking down on a patrol of Viet Cong working their way through the twisting, winding foot trails leading to a base camp they had been sent to gather intelligence. Sergeant O'Francis, Sergeant Skelton, and four Montagnard searched for three days for the camp. All they had to do was follow the patrol to their jungle sanctuary, plot it on a map, work their way to their PZ, be extracted, and let the high-flying "Fly Boys" do their thing. But that would be too easy. Patrols did not always go the way they had been planned. This one was to be no different. One day's travel from discovering a major supply camp, the small patrol ran into a random equally small patrol of Viet Cong at the bottom of a long ridge they had descended. The advantage went to O'Francis and company, as the Viet Cong were not expecting intruders into their concealed world of thick jungle foliage. It was over in minutes, with seven Asian "enemy" dead and one slightly wounded Montagnard.

The men remained out of their vehicle as Jim's ears picked up the sound of another approaching vehicle. He turned his field glasses ever so slightly toward the open gate. Another SUV rose over the steep road leveling off for a few yards at the once stripped job just as it entered through the gate. It paused for a moment and began its approach toward the awaiting party. They moved very slowly. When it came into sight of the tan Blazer, it stopped.

Jim knew that this was not just some of the good 'ole boys meeting on top of the mountain to discuss coon hunting while drinking beers. The smell of something major was about to go down.

The Explorer began its slow approach and stopped some fifty feet from the awaiting men. Three men emerged. Jim could hear their voices but could not determine what they were saying.

The two men in the blazer retrieved a briefcase from the back seat and walked toward their "guests."

One of the three men was standing at the rear of the Explorer. He opened up the hatch and carried a medium-sized black tote bag to the hood. Both parties placed their articles on the hood and examined the other goods. Jim could not see what the items were because of the men's positions but had no problem surmising what it was.

A brief conversation took place, the tote bag was zipped close, and the briefcase was closed. The two men took the tote bag, turned, and began to walk away. The man handling the briefcase turned and walked toward the passenger's side of the Explorer.

One of the men had gotten into the back seat of the Explorer. The third man reached the driver's door, which had been left open. The man in the back seat closed his door. At that point, the two men from the Blazer wheeled around. The one with the tote bag dropped it to the ground. They pulled their weapons from under their light wind-breaker jackets and fired rapidly. The driver and passenger went down instantly.

The man in the back seat quickly opened the door and began firing his 9mm short-barreled Uzi, striking both his attackers and sending them tumbling to the ground.

He then stepped from behind the door and had taken no more than three steps toward the front of the Explorer when one of the two men rose from the ground to his knees and popped off three rounds, hitting his intended target twice in the chest, and once in the abdomen. The intended target sent him wheeling back against the door, forcing it closed as the intended target staggered for two more steps and then flattened face down on the ground.

In a "New York minute," five men lay motionless on the high mountain, flat grassy "strip job."

O'Francis lay motionless as he watched the deal go "south." Twenty minutes passed as he went from one man to the other, examining each body through his field glasses. Looking in both directions from the scene, he saw no one approaching, nor did he hear any approaching vehicles.

It took him another thirty minutes to work his way down onto the "strip job" flat from the natural break in the ridge and the high wall. He moved slowly and cautiously, crouching in the tall grass. The breeze moved the grass back and forth like the waves of an open ocean. Birds began chirping once again. The usual crows flying about seemed to be announcing the "breaking news" events that had occurred, like some on-the-spot reporter broadcasting live on CNN.

Jim stayed close to the high wall taking another ten minutes as he approached the two vehicles. Then, finally went to a low crouching position, almost a crawl, approaching the Explorer first.

He pulled his weapon and paused within ten yards of the vehicle. Although squatting in the thirty-inch high grass, he thought about switching his ammo of "snake" shot to his .357 hollow-point Teflon-tipped ones, but did not.

Instead, he eased to the back of the Explorer and looked at the man who went down last. He laid face down fifteen feet away. The grass concealed him from any further distance. He moved to the man, kneeling on his right knee. Jim checked the pulse on his neck with his left index and middle finger, but nothing. Then, moving methodically, he went to each of the other men who had arrived in the Explorer, checking for signs of life. He found none.

Jim paused for a few moments at the front edge of the Explorer, as he had become aware the crows had stopped their "on the spot broadcasting."

The breeze had picked up slightly, and he sat down, waited, and listened. Ten minutes passed, and the crows began their "broadcasting" again. Finally, Jim became weary, rolled his left leg under him, crossed his right foot over his left leg, placed his right foot flat on the ground, and rose with ease.

Remaining crouched, he moved to the remaining men, both on their backs. They had been hit in the chest area several times, and one had been shot in the right forehead. He felt no pulse from either man.

Looking around, he located the tote bag. The black canvas bag lay a few feet from the feet of the man he had checked first. He reached into the left pocket of his fatigues and pulled out a pair of tan soft leather cowhide gloves.

Replacing his weapon in his shoulder holster, he put his skintight gloves on. Then, moving to the bag, he zipped it open. He saw rectangular brown paper packages, each securely taped. Reaching to his right hip, he retrieved his knife, inserted it into the center of one of the packages, and touched the tip to his tongue.

"Ahh, yes, pure White Snow." He counted the packages. Ten. "Damn!" He spoke softly to himself. "This has to be at least, hell, maybe two, maybe three million on the street. Hell, maybe more. Somebody is going to be really pissed!"

The body of the man who had picked up the briefcase was six feet to the right of the passenger's door. As the bullets had entered his upper back, he had wheeled and stumbled for a few steps and fell. Jim turned and looked over at the man face up. He had not turned loose of the brown leather briefcase. Jim squatted beside the man, removed the case from his hand, walked to the Explorer's passenger's door, opened it, and placed it on the seat. Popping it open, Jim looked down at a lot of neatly wrapped money.

He looked up and through the opposite side of the SUV and then looked around at the bodies on the ground. He picked up one stack and flipped the bills with his thumb, which appeared to be hundreds.

"Holy Shit!" he said softly to himself.

At that point, he knew he could not go down the road he had planned to descend the mountain, so out came the topography map. He thought, getting his bearings; *I need to walk on the edge of the strip job, no trail going through the grass.* He walked directly to the very edge of the "strip job," where it dropped off at a ninety-degree decline, then headed in the opposite direction with the briefcase in hand. He had not gone more than twenty-five yards when he stopped. He backtracked to where he had left the canvas bag, zipped it up, picked it up, and headed east.

He walked more briskly along the flat-stripped grassy terrain making sure he did not make any trail through the tall grasses. Jim traveled for an hour and a half before taking his first break. Sitting on a large boulder, he reviewed his map. Looking up and back down, he figured that two, maybe three, more miles and there should be a hollow leading to the bottom of the mountain.

Talking to himself and tapping his finger on a point on the map, he said, "This should put me about here. Oh well, a few more days in the mountains. I'll need it to think."

Looking back to his map, he figured two more days of moderate trekking would put him home.

He made camp at the top edge of the long hollow leading to the foothills of Copper Ridge.

Making no fire, Jim sat and counted the money stack by stack before darkness fell. Then, after the last stack was counted, he sat looking at the money.

"Christ! Seven hundred and fifty thousand dollars! Damn! Lottery time! There will be more than one somebody pissed!"

Then he looked over at the tote canvas bag, stating in disgust, "Now what in the fuck am I going to do with that shit?" Saying aloud as if he were talking to someone. An hour before dark, Jim got up and walked around the entire area where he had decided to camp for the night.

On the northeast side of the concaved head of the hollow, he carefully removed the topsoil from the side of the hill, placing it to the side. Then, he dug an eighteen-inch hole with his entrenching tool, placed the canvas bag in one of the plastic trash bags he had, and dropped the tote bag in the hole. Covering it up, smoothing the earth, and carefully replacing the topsoil leaving an area as it was naturally.

Then he carefully notated the trees around the area and measured the distance from four different trees, crossing the imaginary line over the buried "Coke." Finally, Jim made notations on the topo map.

He returned to his camp, removed his gloves, ate his dry food, and carefully marked the area on his "topo" map with a grease pencil. Then he enjoyed the sounds of the night residences and the clear star-filled sky until sleep overtook him.

Dawn came at 0530 hours, and he was up with the alarm of birds and, of course, his favorite and the ever clever and observant crows. (As he liked to describe them as the special OP's of the fowl kingdom, FRPs ["flying recon patrols"]. Referencing the famous LRRP's of Viet Nam.)

He placed the money in his backpack and then went three hundred yards down the hollow, where he stopped to dig another hole and placed the empty briefcase in it, taking the same care he had with the hole he had dug for the "coke."

His return home was the usual comments of how bad he smelled and looked. After a long hot shower and a clean shave, he was what Dawn was used to once again.

He was happy to be home. Dawn's ever-present smile and the twinkle in her bright eyes told Jim she was delighted he came home. Her usual "wise-cracking" comments about something just made him smile. He often looked at her and realized how fortunate he was to have her as a soulmate. Her quick wit and sometimes sarcasm did not always sit well with James Patrick. However, that was his mate for life on this planet. And "Twin-flame" forever in the next dimension.

Jim shared his adventure with Dawn, as he knew she could be trusted not to reveal to anyone what had happened.

They had to do some meticulous planning. However, Jim did not know, and could not foresee, and was not forewarned at that time, that his beloved Dawn would be leaving him for a dimension, not of this earth, sending his earthly world back into the darkness he once was in before her loving light had pierced it.

Vultures

John Marshal met Jim at the courthouse at high noon. It was a relatively warm day for October. Jim wore a light blue long-sleeve shirt, a light gray tie, an imprinted fountain pen on the lower tip, khaki Docker slacks, dark blue knee-high socks, and brown loafers. John Marshal wore a dark blue three-piece suit, white shirt, dark blue tie, and black lace-up shoes.

John had arranged to use a conference room off the lobby of the courtroom. It was a small room with one window facing Main Street. A small, well-worn desk and two wooden chairs were in the room.

John took out several files and a law book. He handed James Patrick a file and requested he read it while he went to the restroom.

As Jim read, his blood pressure began to rise. His skin became flushed, and his heart began to increase in beats. Ms. Sheffield had presented John with the copies of the interviews she had with people in her investigation of James Patrick. Unfortunately, her report was not good. According to her sources,

Jim was a terrible person, both in school and out.

Jim had finished the report by the time John returned.

"So, Jim, what do you think?"

"I think..." then he paused, trying to gain his composure.

"I think whoever she got her information from does not like Mr. O'Francis very much. So therefore, I think that this report is spurious."

Then he paused for several moments. John did not say anything. He sat and waited.

"I think the report pisses me off! I hate people to lie about me! I hate people who are afraid to give their names when making statements about me. Well, for that matter, anybody! The point of fact is, John, I am distraught over this! Who are these people? Why can I not have them face me and make these very outlandish, absurd statements?"

John Marshal took his time to answer. He spoke softly.

"Well, I was afraid you would be upset. I did not give this to you to make you upset. But you needed to know what you were about to face with the Department of Social Services.

"In answer to your questions. First, the Social Services do not have to reveal the names of the people who gave them the information. Second, you do not have the right to face your accusers in the world of Social Services. They have their laws."

Jim quickly responded.

"I do not think so, John! Excuse me, Sir, but they cannot be above the law! I am not an attorney, not by a very long shot. However, I know about the government and the state and federal constitutions. I have studied it, taught it."

John smiled. "Jim...yes and no."

Jim responded.

"Yes and no? You cannot have it both ways." Jim protested.

Again, John Marshal smiled at Jim and warmly stated.

"Jim, they have their own set of rules they are allowed to go by. The state legislators are the very people who gave them all this power. Therefore, they can be above the law because it so states. So, Jim, no, they cannot, or are not supposed to be able to convict anyone when the laws of the State of Virginia are in direct conflict with their policies. However, they do, have, and will continue to do so."

Jim expressed himself with anger.

"Well, that is just, excuse me please, fucking great! So, why in the hell are we wasting my time and yours?"

"Because we will win this case, if not here in Reynolds County, then in the hearing of the appeal in Richmond. That is why."

John sat and looked directly at Jim eye to eye, something Jim liked when he met him. He was not afraid to hold eye contact with him.

"Here is how the hearing is going to go. Dear sweet Janet will present all this damaging material in her best, feel sorry for the poor little boy, fashion to the director, Mr. Randy Dowell. Therefore, I do not want you to lose your cool.

I want you to sit and take what she will be stating to the director as fact because she will say that she has done an in-depth and honest investigation into the matter and your background and character. Then, I want you to respond calmly and in a controlled manner when it is your turn to tell your side of the story. You may respond to any of the past-alleged events that you want to. That will be your call.

I do not know any of the details about any of..."
John paused and pointed to the bulky document on
the table given to him by Janet Sheffield, "these very
vague statements about your alleged abuse of
students. She will go into detail when she presents her
case to Randy Dowell. Now can you do that?"

Jim sat and looked hard at John.

"Oh yes, I can do this. The point of fact is John,
there has never been any abuse to any child! I mean
ever! I resent the implications here! If she does go into
this and spouts out details, I want to ask where she got
her information! Also, I want to respond to all child
abuse statements I have been involved in!"

John smiled, "Okay. Well, as I told you, Jim,
you may respond to any statements she makes. But
she will not give you the names of the people she got
the information from."

"So just how does one know if the information
is true, John?"

"Well, they are supposed to conduct a fair and
impartial investigation without biases."

Jim just chuckled..." yea, right! And I am supposed to sit here and believe all that."

"No, I didn't say you had to believe it. It is just what the Department of Social Services will tell you. But moreover, they will stick to what they say. They will not change."

"Well hell, John, with what is in that report, along with the details, it is already a damn lie! The report is tainted from the very get-go!"

"I know. I believe you. I am on your side. I do not take every case that crosses my desk, Jim. But that is not the point here. You handle this like a professional. She will expect you to go off. That is what she is hoping for Jim.

"Sweet Janet is mad as a wet hen because you were acquitted of the assault charges. Again, we have blown holes in the stories these students have portrayed as facts. Now again, bear in mind, this did not sit well with sweet Janet."

"Well, I have one thing to say about sweet Janet. Get a real-life! Let me get just one more thing out of my system before we gladiators adjourn to the arena.

"Janet and her cohorts do not have a FUCKING clue about what it is like to be a teacher in a public school system and deal with these insubordinate, rude, impolite thuds!

"And also, these types of students are in the rural areas, not just in the city school that you hear about on TV. Sweet Janet lives in a world that does not exist! She is a total idiot!" Then Jim took a deep breath and smiled. "Damn, I feel much better having said that."

Then James P. stood. "Okay. I will handle this thing. You do not have to worry. Hell, I will not blow the case. I work better under pressure anyway. Trust me, John, on this one."

Then he smiled again and looked at his watch. "I am ready. Let's go to battle."

As they entered a room twenty by forty feet, to their right along the wall sat Sweet Janet Sheffield. Unfortunately, the chair where she was seated was not big enough for her obese frame. Moreover, her muu-muu attire did nothing for her appearance. Her hair was a dirty blond color and shabby, looking as if it needed to be washed and styled. *Maybe I can get her an appointment at the Cut and Style hair salon. Gees. I am sure that either Denise or Alice could make her look presentable,* James P. thought.

To Janet's right was the same man who accompanied her at the assault trial.

Mr. Randy Dowell placed a chair in the middle between the chairs to his left and right.

"Good afternoon, gentlemen."

"Good afternoon, Mr. Dowell. I want to introduce James Patrick O'Francis."

"Mr. Dowell," Jim responded as he nodded his head. James P. refused to shake his hand.

Mr. Dowell then introduced Janet and Edward Houston. He was a well-built man, five-ten or eleven, one hundred and eighty pounds, dressed casually, with tan slacks, a white shirt, blue tie, and brown slip-on shoes.

Again, Jim only nodded toward them. Dowell instructed them to have a seat. All introductions were done as a professional courtesy for O'Francis, as John knew all of them, and they knew him from previous cases. He had to defend teachers from the ever-ravaging vultures of Social Services.

After a few moments of preliminaries, Randy Dowell instructed Janet to begin her report. Janet's story rolled out like a Steven King horror novel. Her portrayal of O'Francis made Pope Paul II look like Hannibal Lector.

"Sweet" Janet's report revealed how abusive James Patrick had been to athletes and students.

O'Francis, according to Janet, had struck male students physically and had, in the course of breaking up fights between students, used unreasonable and unnecessary force to do so. In addition, she stated he was accused of mentally abusing students in his classes. Janet stated for the official record that his conduct outside of school was just as abusive.

"Sweet" Janet went into detail about each indictment. She then went into the events of 5 April, weaving a story even better than the students had in court. She had a lot more practice at storytelling. Jim tried to humor himself with his thoughts.

She should write a fuck'en book! This fictional storyline is as good as a Steven King novel. She would make a Fuck'en fortune. At least she would be leaving teachers alone.

At the end of the thirty-minute report, she stated that Mr. O'Francis had terrorized several teachers and several of his supervisors. Several principals had indicated that they feared for their very lives. She reported that he had even sued one of his principals. "Sweet" Janet stated that she had gone to the courthouse to obtain the case records, but they were missing.

She implied that Mr. O'Francis had been able to get rid of the files from the court records.

Ms. Sheffield concluded that several of the people she spoke with had warned her that she was putting her life in grave danger by investigating O'Francis.

Then she twisted and turned in her seat, as best she could, arched her shoulders back as if she had just presented the world with the facts that would win her the Pulitzer Prize in Literature.

James Patrick sat very erect in his most uncomfortable chair, feet flat on the floor, and his hands cupped together in his lap through it all without making a sound. He had not moved his body in any manner. Jim sat like a stone statue. He had not made any expressions on his face, and he had looked directly at Janet the entire time she presented her report. He was aware that Mr. Houston, her associate, he presumed, seated directly across from him, was watching his every move, which was part of the grand scheme of the SS department.

Mr. Dowell took a few seconds before he addressed Mr. Marshal.

"Mr. Marshal, would you like to respond to any of the reports presented here today by Mrs. Sheffield?"

"Well, Janet certainly portrayed my client as a villainous person. I truly am surprised that he is still working for Reynolds County School System. But, in all fairness, Mr. Dowell, I would like to let Mr. O'Francis respond to any or all of the alleged and unbiased statements Ms. Sheffield has obtained from her unbiased investigation. He would have more insight into all these improprieties and illegal acts than I would."

John then turned his head to his left.

"Mr. O'Francis, you may respond to any of the statements or just tell your side of the story that took place the day of the incident we are here for."

O'Francis took his time and looked at each of the Social Service people present.

"Well, I would first like to respond to some of the allegations Ms. Sheffield has presented to you today, Mr. Dowell."

"You may make any statements you wish, Mr. O'Francis." Mr. Dowell stated.

"Thank you, sir." Jim crossed his right leg over his left, cupping his hands on his lap.

"First and foremost, Mr. Dowell, Ms. Sheffield received false information from someone, or she has misquoted whomever she got the information from. Or the other option is she fabricated all of her testimony. If I may, Mr. Dowell, I would like to ask a question."

"You may." He nodded as he spoke.

"Ms. Sheffield, where did you obtain this information presented here today?"

She squirmed in her seat and moved her shoulders back and forth.

"I am not at liberty to give you that information."

"Well, that tells me a lot. I had heard that same statement from the person you obtained all of this information many times before, which was the typical response from the person you got your information when he was telling one of his lies."

"Mr. O'Francis..."

Jim cut Janet off.

"Ma'am, you had your turn to make all the statements you wanted. It is my turn to respond to them without being interrupted."

Sheffield frowned at Jim and moved her upper body back and forth aggressively.

"I have never mistreated a student! I have never mistreated an athlete! I have never struck a student or an athlete. Never have I injured a student when breaking up any fight. This is more than I can say for Damon Bales, your main source of information, Ms. Sheffield, who, for the record, broke a student's shoulder and also slapped a student at a football game when he disrespectfully spoke to him with a multitude of witnesses. He also addressed the student and the two other students accompanying him with several sentences of very colorful metaphors. I have no doubts that most if not all of your information came from Bales and or any one of his loyal allies."

James P. O'Francis deliberately paused for three minutes to get his thoughts in order.

Then, Jim continued calmly with less sternness in his voice.

"Now, if you had asked the right people who were with me during my coaching years, you would have found out that the information you have presented here today depicting my character was not who I am. That would also apply to the classroom colleagues. Instead, I believe that you sought your answers from people who have, over the years, slandered as well as libeled my name! By all appearances here today with your report, they still are! I believe that is what you were looking to find. Then you found it. The people you have sought to give you the information you wanted are mendacious dissembling and have one goal—to discredit my name! Destroy my career. Your policy here in this state-run department is an autocratic one!"

Jim intentionally had another short pause in his rebuttal.

Janet's face was becoming red, and she twisted more in her seat. Her face became more distorted.

Edward remained calm, showing no emotion to anything James P. said.

"Now to a few specifics. I have broken up a few fights in my day. Never have I been charged with any wrongdoing in any of them. I did the job as I was required to do as a teacher in this county and by the school's policy manual. Therefore, your information is tainted!"

Janet started to speak. Jim just held up his arm, four figures folded, and index finger extending upward to indicate that he was not finished.

"There was one fact you presented here today that was the truth. I did sue a principal. Now that, you did get correct, Ms. Sheffield. I sued Damon Clay Bales and Richard Finkel for libel and slander."

"Excuse me, Mr. O'Francis, for interrupting," Mr. Dowell stated. "What does any of this have to do with what went on with you and this boy at the, ahh, whatever it is?"

"Alternative School, and it has absolutely nothing to do with it, Sir."

"Then let's just get to the incident you are charged with."

"No problem, Sir, I was just responding to these absurd allegations that Ms. Sheffield has presented to you depicting my character and my past and, as she has stated, using her very words, showing a pattern of behavior. And before I go to the incident of 5 April, I would like to state, Mr. Dowell, that I can and would present witnesses to any of these alleged events you allowed Ms. Sheffield to present openly here today."

James P. took another 90-second pause to control the narrative being spun. He also knew most people dislike long delays in conversations or testimonies.

"Now to the events of 5 April…" Jim went through the entire events that had occurred just as he had in court and just as he had written up in his documentation.

After he had finished, Edward requested to ask Jim a question.

"Mr. O'Francis. If you were to have to do it all over, would you have handled the matter differently?"

"Knowing what I know now? Yes!"

"Do you think this has changed you as a teacher?"

"Yes!"

"In what way?" Mr. Edwards inquired.

At that, Jim paused for a full minute. He never took his eyes off Mr. Edwards. James Patrick felt he was being set up with the question. Then he slowly answered Edwards' question.

"I think, as of now, I will not ever get involved with any type of confrontation with a student. I will not be the caring person I have been in the past. Caring, as far as concern, for the welfare of the students."

At that, John Marshal interjected before any more questions were asked. He presented the legal side of the issue to the local Social Service board. John gave each party a copy of the written law concerning Bruce McCloud and James Patrick O'Francis.

After hearing his statement, pointing out what the laws of the State of Virginia had on its books and the policies of the county school system, Janet Sheffield made a statement that stunned Jim.

"Mr. Marshal, these laws or school policies do not apply to Social Services' policies."

John Marshal broke a smile.

"Ms. Sheffield, these laws apply to all people in the State of Virginia. No other law or policy can supersede the laws of the state. And the state laws cannot supersede the laws of the United States."

"Well, Mr. Marshal, that may be true, but they do not apply to our policies. We have our policies that we go by."

"Mr. Dowell, I have given you legal room to find my client innocent of these charges if you so desire. Again, we thank you for your time today. We'll be in touch."

John Marshal looked at Jim. His eyes told O'Francis that it was time to leave. He rose from his chair, John was already standing, and they walked out of the room.

They rode in silence to where Jim had his truck parked before O'Francis said anything.

"John, is Sheffield as stupid as she presented herself today?"

"Yes."

"John, I have taught political science for many years, and I do not think that any law or policy can supersede the laws of a state and so on up the line."

"You are correct. They cannot."

"Look, I hope I did alright in there today... I did not know what to say about all the bullshit she

presented. I mean, bullshit is an understatement.
There is no way, John...believe me...no way that any of
that shit is true! John, allegations like that are
precisely why I sued Damon Bales!"

"Not to worry, Jim. You did well. You have the
right to defend yourself from all the allegations, as did
you with Bruce attacking you. Remember, he hit you.
You did not hit him. The law gives you due deference.
O'Francis, that is the law despite what "Sweet" Janet
would like to think."

"I do not know, John. I have a bad feeling
here."

"Look, even if they do find you guilty, we have
the right to appeal to Richmond. They do have some
knowledge of the law there. You will be alright. I think
we will win in the long haul. Okay. Now don't worry
yourself about this. We'll be alright. Trust me,
O'Francis. Trust me."

Jim shook his head. "Okay, I will. You know I
have little faith in our judicial system."

"Ahh, but wait, my fine Irish friend. The
system did right by you in the assault charges. Right?
I mean, you told the truth, and the judge saw it was
the truth. Right?"

"Yeah, you're right on that one, and I will give credit where it is due. Are these people that ignorant?"

John smiled. "Ah yes. How ignorant, you asked? Well, you saw for yourself today. This case is not the first time I have had to dance with these people. The very same ones with a case much harder than yours, and in the end, they lost, and we won."

"You had to appeal to the state?" Jim asked.

"Yes. O'Francis, the state board personally looks at both sides' facts without bias and more objectively in Richmond than they do here in Reynolds County. Believe me."

The two parted with John Marshal telling James Patrick that he would be in contact with him and that if he had any questions or anything was bothering him, he could call him at his office or his home anytime he wanted or needed to.

Deliverance

Jim arrived at his office at his usual time of 8:20. His official time started at 8:30 A.M., but that was a pile of buffalo dung for him, as his hours did not reflect that of a regular teacher.

Sometimes he arrived at 9:00, sometimes at 10:00 A.M.; however, when the typical teacher was at home in the late afternoon, Jim was still working. Sometimes at 7:00 P.M., he was leaving a student's house and headed for the office to swap out the very used county car he had nicknamed *"The Blue Goose"* for his black Nissan truck, nicknamed *"The Crow."*

Jim had two students on this day, one on the far western end of the county, a thirty-five-minute drive from the central office, and one on the county's eastern end, a 45-minute drive from his office.

By the time he left his morning student, he had stopped by the high school on the western end of the county and had delivered his students' work to the student's teachers. Then he drove to the high school on the eastern end of the county, got his students' work from the teachers and prepared for his afternoon student.

The school year had only three weeks left in it— a year Jim would like to forget.

It had been over a month since the incident at the Alternative School, and O'Francis faced yet another major battle to keep his name and teaching profession intact. He was well aware of the forces at work to permanently dismantle him from teaching. Yet, why certain people were so obsessed with his destruction troubled him. He was a simple teacher trying to enlighten his students, expand their minds.

However, he tried to keep an upbeat attitude, as he was also well aware that the students he had to see had no clue about his problems. For most of them, the issues they had were of significant proportion. Little did they know what life was going to throw at them? Then they would look back at their teens and think, it had not been a problem.

He arrived back at the office from his morning student at 1:00 P.M. He took all the needed material from the light blue county car, "*The Blue Goose*," and put it on the floor and seat of the passenger's side of "*The* Crow."

It took a four-wheel-drive vehicle to get up to the top of the mountain where his afternoon student lived. Jim surmised that only his superintendent, "LT," as he referred to her, appreciated what he did for the student he was assigned.

When he was finished with his afternoon student, he would go straight to his home and to his adorable wife.

Melissa Casey was yet another one of the girls pregnant and was allowed to go homebound for medical reasons. Something Jim disapproved of, but he would say nothing. He did his job as assigned, like the good "soldier" he was.

In one of our conversations concerning the military, Jim stated, "It is not for us to ask why but to do and die." A Marine saying Jim would say. "Even though I was not a "jar-head," as he referred to them.

I always heard them called "Leather-necks," I said to Jim as he related this part of his life.

"The same. There is a story behind each nickname. But for another time." Jim replied.

He had been going to Melissa's home for six weeks and learned much about her home life. Her mother did a lot of talking to Jim O'Francis, who was an excellent listener.

His first trip to the house was a trip in itself. Six miles east of Honsburg, turn right on route 614, go one mile, and turn right on the first dirt road you come to. Follow that road up the mountain until you enter the "strip job." Travel right out the "strip job" for about a mile, turn left up the hill off the strip job for another mile, and follow that road until you come to the old home place. Turn left as you enter the gate and go a quarter of a mile to the trailer.

Now the trailer was set on top of a ridge overlooking an array of magnificent mountains. Jim stood and admired the view and thought it would make a place for a lovely home, but that was not the case. The old home place was, by all appearances, at least seventy-five years old.

To quote Jim in this part of his story:

"Now, people, in general, think that the movie Deliverance was just a movie, but a point of fact is, there are many places in the Appalachian Mountains that are like the people in the movie. Mountain people. Nothing wrong with mountain people, you understand. But, again, the point of fact is, I like them. Well, for the most part. One has just got to learn what type of people you are dealing with. Adjust and overcome."

Jim had learned much about the broken family he was now visiting weekly. The mother, Lara, had left her husband, Bob, or rather it would be best to phrase it, Bob returned to his home place to stay with his mother.

Bob was an abusive husband and drank more often than he should. He would be working on his "toys," motorcycles, Harley-Davidsons, in an old shed, what appeared to be a garage, each time Jim went by the home place on his way to the trailer. Bob would be playing music from the sixties, which was not all bad for Jim. He looked to be in his late thirties and, by all appearances, someone caught in a time warp from the late sixties or early seventies.

O'Francis arrived at the trailer at 2:30 in the afternoon. Melissa had two tests, which would take up the afternoon session. By three-thirty, she had finished the first test. Lara had expressed concern about Bob coming to the trailer several times as he had been drinking all day. O'Francis paid little attention to the comments that Lara had made.

After Melissa finished her first test, Lara exited the trailer to the front porch to smoke a cigarette. Melissa got a glass of water and looked out the kitchen window. O'Francis sensed both women were on edge a few minutes after his arrival. Melissa returned to the dining room table, and a look of fear had taken over her face.

"Mr. O'Francis, when daddy is drunk, he is very violent. So I don't think it is safe for you to be here today. I am so very sorry."

"Melissa," Jim stated in a calm and firm voice.

"Not to worry about things you have no control over. You have enough to worry about with the baby you are carrying. You are a month, maybe two, the doctor said, correct?" She nodded her head to confirm.

"Well, you worry about the next test we have to take, and do not worry about Mr. O'Francis. Okay?"

Jim reviewed all material that was to have been on the test before Melissa began to take the rather long test. He was sure that the same test was not given to the students in the regular classroom, but he had no control over that, and he did not worry himself over the fact that teachers had no concern about the students Jim had been assigned homebound. Jim ensured they knew the material well enough that it did not matter what type or how long of a test the teachers chose to give. They would pass it.

Thirty minutes passed, and Lara came into the kitchen.

"Mr. O'Francis, Bob is coming, and he is drunk. So I think you should leave. I don't mean to offend you, but he is not very nice when drunk."

"Mrs. Casey, I will do so as soon as Melissa finishes her test. It will only take a short while. Her education is critical. Do not worry yourself about me."

A few minutes passed, and Bob came into the living room of the relatively old trailer, with a large addition added to the living room and bedrooms. Lara kept it clean inside and had her home in order and items neat and in what appeared to be their proper place. It had a clean smell, which O'Francis was glad, for there were some houses he had to go to that the odors would gag a maggot.

Lara began pleading with Bob to leave, saying that Melissa's teacher was present and that she had to take a test. She tried to get him to understand that her education was important. Bob was the typical "backwoods redneck" mountain man who was mean when drunk. He was the type that would cut you with a knife without a second thought. The kind you saw in a bar that wanted to take on anyone and everyone after a few drinks. The type of person that could spoil a person's beer when all one wanted was to be left alone to have a cold one and go. Most people call Bob's type of person a "mean ass-hole drunk!"

Bob started into the kitchen. Lara tried to step in front of him, but with no success. Melissa had stopped taking her test. Tears welled up in her eyes, running down her cheeks.

O'Francis slowly moved his legs from under the table and positioned himself to where he could rise without having the table to contend with.

The kitchen was relatively small. The table, old, chrome legs, looked like the type you saw in homes in the late fifties and early sixties. Four matching chairs with chrome legs and plaid seats and backs. A brown-colored refrigerator to Jim's right and a sink with a small amount of counter space to Jim's rear. One window over the sink and one beside the table where O'Francis and Melissa were sitting.

Bob walked into the kitchen. At that moment, Jim knew he had but one choice: take him out before he could strike his first blow. He had seen Bob's type so many times in his earlier days when he made his rounds to the local bars in the towns and cities he had traveled.

As Bob approached, O'Francis saw in his eyes that he intended to show him what a "bad-ass" he was and set a tone for future visits, if at all.

Jim came out of his chair like a bolt of lightning, driving his left extended fingers into Bob's throat. Both of Bob's hands instantly went to his throat as he gasped for air. Bob's knees were slightly bent, and Jim drove his open right hand like the back edge of a knife upward into his groin. His left hand now firmly grasped Bob's shirt at his upper chest, lifting him upward and back with force against the wall beside the refrigerator.

Jim moved close to Bob's right ear and whispered, "Do not ever threaten me! I couldn't give a good god damn what you do up on this fucking mountain, or for that matter, anywhere else. But do not ever, never, ever, threaten me!"

As Jim whispered in his ear, he had rolled his right hand over to grasp Bob's testicles and squeezed them. Bob was still struggling to get his breath.

"I am not your little chicken shit Reynolds County teacher! When I leave this fucking mountain today, this event had better stay up on this

mountain! You understand me, Bob! I have nothing personal against you. Let's me and you leave it at that!"

Jim let go of Bob's shirt and testicles. Bob dropped to the floor on his knees, still gasping for air. Jim turned to Melissa. "You finish the test later or tomorrow whenever you feel like it."

She spoke with a "crackling" voice, tears streaming down her cheeks. "But aren't you supposed to be here when I take the test?" she stated.

"Yes. I was here. As far as completing your test, you let me worry about that. Just use the honor system is all I ask."

He gathered up the file case he had made that contained his students' records and walked into the living room.

As he passed Lara, standing at the kitchen entrance with her eyes the size of golf balls, James Patrick O'Francis paused.

"Sorry, Mrs. Casey, but I had no choice. I hope you understand. If you do not want me to return for next week's session, just call the office and let me know. You all have a nice day."

All Lara did was nod her head and then smile.

O'Francis walked through the living room and spoke as he exited the trailer, "Melissa, I will see you next week, okay? You work hard for me."

"Okay, Mr. O'Francis, I will. Thanks." Still with a slight crackle in her young teen voice.

As Jim walked onto the porch, he spoke loud enough so Bob could hear him, "I really like your Harleys. You play good music also, Bob. Maybe we can talk about sixties music in the next few weeks."

He walked forty feet to his truck, put his file case on the floorboard of the passenger's side, then walked to the driver's side and got in. He then unzipped a section of his soft brown leather case sitting on the passenger's seat, pulled out his Smith & Wesson .380 automatic, and set it beside him. Next, he started the truck, pushed in a tape by Bob Seger, took the time to load his pipe and then lit it, took a few puffs to get it going, then backed out of the dirt driveway to a wide spot, turned the truck around and slowly drove down the mountain. He smiled as he thought of what had taken place.

Then he talked aloud to himself.

"Just ain't going to happen again. Never! Adult, teen, male, female. Just ain't going ever to happen again!"

Then he started singing along with Bob Seger, *"STOOD THERE BOLDLY; SWEATING IN THE SUN; FELT LIKE A MILLION; FELT LIKE NUMBER ONE..."*

State Legislators

After the scheduled state social service board meeting in Richmond, O'Francis's decisive victory, and the severe reprimand to "Sweet Janet," the two men celebrated lunch together, with Jim dubbing John Marshal the "Dragon Killer."

However, "Sweet Janet" was bitter and hated O'Francis with every breath she took. Unknown to all in the Department of Social Services, she covertly entered James Patrick O'Francis' name into the national database as a child abuser, which would remain for seven years. James P. would not learn of this illegal covert action for over a year. In the interim, O'Francis, being a Political Science minded person, James P. was working on a bill to present to the Convention of teachers for approval. Jim once again had been elected as a delegate from his area. If, after his presentation to the body of over two thousand teachers, they voted to approve, the proposed bill would then be sent to the State Legislative body. Two thousand teachers voted unanimously to allow his bill to move forward.

After going through committee discussion and if passed, the proposed bill made it to the floor for a vote to pass or fail a law that would prevent the Social Service department from unjustly walking into a school and declaring a teacher to be charged with any child abuse, physical or mental.

James Patrick O'Francis's day of reckoning was upon him. He stood before the Virginia State Delegate committee on the proposed legislative action. He had three minutes.

Bets were taken by members of the "great minds" of the Richmond Teachers Association staff that he would fail.

James presented his case before the board of nine delegates. Afterward, he stood in front of the podium and microphone in silence. There was a longer-than-normal pause at the end of his presentation. Then a series of questions from five of the nine delegates proceeded. And the conversation of Q & A's lasted ten minutes.

To the surprise of all the "elites" from the Richmond Central office, the committee agreed to take his case under advisement and referred it to a sub-committee.

The following day James P. presented his case to the Virginia State Senators. James P.'s Senate representative Phillip Pritchet from Liberty, was present as he addressed the twelve Senators. He was given five minutes to plead his case. His five minutes turned into fifteen minutes. Again, James P. was victorious, and the Senate committee agreed to address his issue in a sub-committee.

James P. learned that his proposed bill was made law several months later.

The Yellow House

Ranard Wolffe enjoyed an evening of drinking and sex with another of his women who, legally by social standards, belonged to another man. However, Ranard had no morals in addition, nor did the women. They had spent the greater part of the night consuming alcohol, watching X-rated movies, and partaking in their form of sex.

At 2:00 A.M. Ranard's phone rang. On the fifth ring, he managed to roll over and reach to his nightstand to drag it from the receiver.

"Hello," Ranard answered with a groggy voice, his eyes still closed, his head on the pillow.

"Ranard, this is Marshy."

"Who?" Ranard replied, still not fully awake. His body was recovering from all the alcohol he had consumed and the sex he had with a woman fifteen years younger.

"God damn it, I said this is La Mar Marshy! Now wake your ass up and talk to me!"

The voice registered in his mind, and his eyes opened wide and quickly. He sat up in bed as if someone had suddenly fired a gun into the air.

"La Mar." Ranard looked at the clock on his nightstand. "What are you calling me at, ahh, damn, 2:05 in the morning?"

"I need your assistance."

"Okay, what?" Ranard answered obediently.

"I am in the Princeton jail. I need you to come to bail me out. Now!"

There was a long pause on the phone, and the silence left Marshy thinking no one was on the other end of the line. "Ranard, you there?"

"Yes, Sir. I am here. Just, ahh, what..."

He did not get to finish his question. "Look, don't ask. Just get your ass up here as soon as possible and get me out!"

"Yes, Sir. I will be there in, ahh, just as soon as I can." Then he hung the phone up. The twenty-five-year-old teacher, whose husband had gone on a fishing trip for a week, rolled over and inquired about what was happening. Ranard informed her he had to leave for a few hours to take care of some emergency business.

Aileen rolled back over on her right side. "Okay."

Ranard got dressed and was on his way in ten minutes. However, getting to the jail would take him an hour and a half.

Linda Diamond had bought the large Victorian home in 1981 and had refurbished it in grand style. Linda was a self-made millionaire and had moved to the small city to open a business she had longed to operate all her adult life. She painted her house yellow and nicknamed it the "Yellow House." She ran her house of prostitution with classy women she had imported from the northern city of New Jersey. Her high prices catered to the surrounding area's upper-middle-class and wealthy clientele. They arrived at the "Yellow House" by appointment only.

The reverend Paul Lina and his Bible-thumping Evangelical Southern Baptist congregation had been politically putting pressure on the Mayor and the city council for ten years to close the tax-paying "Yellow House" down. However, he had little success, as Ms. Diamond had been a significant financial contributor to the Mayor and several council members elected to power. In addition, Ms. Diamond played the political game well and knew what it took to keep her business open. As a result, her clients were well shielded from the public and any scandals.

Nevertheless, the pressure had been mounting, and the Mayor and the police department had to raid the "Yellow House," temporarily shutting it down and getting the non-taxpaying Christian organization off their backs.

Even though ninety-ninety percent were as hypocritical as the day is long, which was quite normal for the sounding area. Ms. Diamond had been pre-warned as to when the raid would take place. Linda Diamond made sure that none of the affluent local clientele would be present on the night of the "surprise" raid on her business.

The ten women she had working for her were also informed about what would be taking place and were prepared for the police when they arrived. On the other hand, the clients present were not enlightened about the mock raid and were arrested along with all the working women.

Ms. Linda Diamond had her attorney, Ms. Anna Chemali Stengel, AKA "AC," and her law firm, Stengel and McKenzie, on quick dial twenty-four-seven-three-sixty-five. When La Mar was allowed to make his one call, Linda Diamond had her women out on bail and back at the "Yellow House."

Ranard Wolffe arrived one hour and twenty minutes after La Mar's call. He posted bail, and they were on their way by five o'clock. After picking up La Mar's car, they stopped at a coffee house in Blue Ridge.

The server came up to them in a matter of minutes after arriving. "May I get you gentlemen something?"

"Coffee, please," La Mar informed her.

"So, La Mar, what the hell happened?" Ranard inquired.

"Hell, I don't know. One minute I was having a good time; the next thing I knew, all hell broke loose.

Son of a bitch, Ranard, I thought you said this place was safe?"

"Well, it is. I have been going there, off and on, for several years, and nothing bad like this ever happened. The woman who ran the place assured me that I would be safe. No one would ever know. Hell, it is a professionally run place."

Several minutes passed without either one speaking. Within minutes the server brought their coffee and left. The two men sat and sipped their hot coffee in total silence.

Then La Mar broke the silence. "Damn! Five hundred for the whore."

Ranard interrupted La Mar, "They are called ladies of the evening."

"I don't care what they are called. Plus, seven hundred for bail. What the hell will the fine be? We have to keep this quiet! Understand! I may need your help on this."

"Not a problem, I'll help you. Ain't no one going to find out? Too far from home. Where is Sandy?"

"Ahh, she is gone to some kind of conference in Richmond."

After thirty minutes of conversation and planning, they parted to their homes, another hour's drive.

Labor Day

I had driven by the O'Francis home several times to see where he lived and how. I had never stopped by for a visit nor requested to come by for a visit. Being the old journalist I am, I just more or less wanted to see things for myself and make a judgment call on observation.

It had been a while since I had talked to Jim, and I had made myself aware of some of the problems he was encountering with the school system and social services.

Being a veteran journalist, I established several contacts in Reynolds County. After extensive research, it amazed me how someone so dedicated to the betterment of his students got in so much trouble. What further surprised me was that the school system's leadership did not see his positive, productive work. They sure were quick to see and react to anything controversial surrounding O'Francis. Yet he stood his ground against whomever.

I made up my mind to go for a visit. Just drop in without notice. I entered the section of town Jim and Dawn lived in and stopped as I approached where Hickman turned into Maple. Up the street, I saw O'Francis laboring away. I backed my Jeep up to a wide spot on the street and decided to observe for a few minutes. I got my camera and snapped a few pictures of him laboring. He was carrying the remains of a tree, which appeared to have been recently cut. From where I sat, I could see the remains of a stump next to his privacy fence. The line of seventy-five-foot tall pine trees lined the boundary of his land along Maple Street and extended from the fence 200 hundred feet to the front section of his property.

I sat and watched him haul an entire tree to some point at the back of his house. I could only see him enter his privacy gate, which he had secured open, and walk toward the hill to the back of his home. He went back and forth, first the trunk, which had been cut into what appeared to be about four-foot lengths. Then, he would heave them upon his shoulder, and one by one, he would haul them to some point on the hill, then all the limbs and small branches. All this took a bit of time. Finally, after he had what appeared to me, at any rate, finished, he came to the street with a shop broom and swept the street clean of all small scrap pieces from the tree.

I shook my head. Thinking, *who in the hell would take the time to clean the street after they spent close to an hour carrying an entire tree off the side?*

I told myself I would ask him that very question. It was a little after 10:00 A.M. I felt it was time for a brief visit.

As I entered his driveway, his wife Dawn was hanging clothes on the line to the north side of their house. I had never met her, and I heard her call for Jim, informing him that "someone was here." However, she did not seem overly joyous.

I was aware of their exclusion, even with neighbors. His corner lot with large pine trees covering Maple Street and halfway up Pine Street with a large holly bush, seven feet high and six feet in diameter, helped immensely.

Jim came from the back of their home. His Notre Dame tee shirt was soaked with sweat, and his black headband, which had been cut out of a black tee shirt, a strip of cloth about thirty-six inches long, was tied at the back of his head with tails of some six to eight inches long, hanging down onto his upper back, also soaked in sweat.

He had a bottle of water in his right hand. He wore gray shorts, white socks, and brown ankle-high work boots. I began getting out of the jeep as soon as I saw him. A smile crossed his face as soon as he saw me.

"Hey, John Frederick," he exclaimed with a joyful, warm voice. "Come in, my good friend."

"I assume it will be safe for me to park here."

"Yeah, sure. Hell, we ain't going anywhere."

"I mean your sign."

O'Francis looked at the four-by-four posts holding the cross-post, with four cloth lines attached.

The sign read, "*If you are not Irish, your vehicle will be towed away.*"

"Oh yes, you are safe." Then he turned as Dawn walked to his side. I had walked within six feet of them.

"Dawn, this is John Frederick O'Donovan."

"Oh, are we a wee bit of Irish also?" She spoke in her best Irish brogue, which was quite good.

"Oh yes. Just a wee bit," I replied with a smile.

Then they walked me to the back of their home, where he had built a rather large deck that extended fifty-five feet long and ten feet wide along the edge of their home. As I walked to the far end of the deck and turned to look upon slopping topography behind Jim and Dawn's home, wanting to see where Jim had been hauling the cut tree, I saw another huge deck setting some hundred feet toward the top of the incline, that he called his hill. Pine trees surrounded his property. On the sloping terrain, a large pine grove was extended out from the backside of his deck.

"Nice place you have here, Jim. You think you have enough decks?" He laughed.

"Ahh, probably not. And I thank you for the compliment. We like it. It has taken us thirty years to get it the way we want. But I have enjoyed working on it."

"May we walk up there?" As I pointed to the deck on the hill.

"Sure."

He had stone steps leading from the deck we were on and stone steps leading up to a large deck.

After getting to the twenty-five-foot squared deck, I could see what he had done with the cut tree.

Between the pine trees lining the top of the sloped land at the edge of the bank where the landscape dropped twenty feet to the street below, and between the pine trees that lined the top of the bank, he built a brush fence. The barrier was three feet high and extended entirely around the exterior of his property.

"Jim, I have to ask you a question."

"Okay."

"Why were you sweeping the street?"

"Oh, that. Well, you see, "County" and his nephew, Lloyd, two former students, helped me cut down a huge pine tree that had died. I asked the power company to cut it, as I was afraid it would fall onto the electrical lines. However, as usual, big companies have little time for the everyday consumer. Shit, John, I called them in April. Anyway, David, Lloyd, and I cut it down into sections. David hooked a long rope to his truck, then attached it to the upper section of the tree. As Lloyd would notch each one, David would ease his truck up the street, and the sections would just miss the power lines as they fell. We finished the cutting late yesterday evening.

Well, all that had to be cleaned up. I did not get to it until this morning. The street had many little tiny bits and pieces scattered all over the fucking place. It looked terrible, and besides, I made the mess. I needed to clean it up. You know what I mean?"

"Yes, I do." Then I smiled at Jim.

"Have you had lunch?" he asked me.

"Well. No, but..."

He cut me off. "There will be no buts. I will see if Dawn can fix us a little bit to eat."

By eleven-thirty, we were eating. The lunch lasted for two hours. Dawn was the perfect host. Jim, Dawn, and I sat in the tranquility of his back deck and talked about the joys of life. Of course, I had to answer a load of questions from Dawn concerning myself, which I found rather enjoyable. I learned another critical trait about Jim. He did not talk much when Dawn took the stage. She dominated the discussions. She would have made one hell of a reporter. I found her intellect challenging, humor extremely joyful, and wit sharp. I invited her to accompany Jim sometimes on one of his retreats to my home on my mountain top. She accepted.

Religious Sects of the World

Jim's World Geography class was about to begin the section on world religions. He did not know how his junior high students would react to the information he presented, which was part of the core curriculum. He realized that the material he was about to introduce and pass on knowledge of was the same material he had been forbidden ever to teach again, according to Damon C. "Himmler" Bales, the head of the La Mar "Gestapo" at Honsburg High.

As Jim sat at his desk looking at the board a good 30 minutes before his first junior high student would walk through the door, he thought back on one of many infamous days in Bales's office. However, this was not Bales's school.

Would the parents of the junior high students file a complaint with Wolffe, and would he have to go through yet another round of why he should not be teaching the students the world's major religions? Was it worth the stress of fighting the administration and some of the more narrow-minded people in the community? Blinded by the dogmas of religious propaganda, they had been programmed to believe. He talked to himself, *"Religion is the opium of the mindless masses of the world."*

Was passing along knowledge that important at this point in his teaching career? He recalled that insane encounter that no one would have ever believed with his high school principal.

It was the start of just another week for O'Francis as he prepared himself for whatever Bales and his disciples would throw at him. Then, just as the first period began and his freshman and sophomore students entered his World Geography class, the PA system came on, and Belinda was on the other end.

"Mr. O'Francis."

"Yes."

"Mr. O'Francis, Mr. Bales wants to see you in his office during your planning period."

"Okay, thank you, Ms. Bookmann."

Jim's planning period was the second period, and he knew his trip to the office was not one of congratulations. Jim could not think of what he was to have done wrong, according to "someone," however, it did not make any difference. It could simply be that he had farted incorrectly.

Then he smiled to himself and began his second week of lecturing his students about the major religions of the world, which included maps, diagrams, and charts of the history of each. He never included the dogmas or cannons of any aspect of the world's major religions.

He usually likes to make it a one-week section, but he did not finish because of all the interruptions that had taken place the previous week. So he had two more days of notes to give, one day for review, and two tests, one note test, and one map and chart test, which covered his week in world geographies major religions.

Jim had noticed that the interest in the subject had perked up with several lackadaisical students, which excited him as more and more questions were being asked concerning all the different religions. Of course, he was aware of the religious propaganda that permeated the entire region and prevented young minds from becoming independently thinking adults.

James Patrick would present them with some facts, and maybe it would spark enough interest that a few would become thinkers and not blindly follow what "someone" who claimed that "God" or "Jesus" had deemed them the messenger of the "word."

He quit his lecture three minutes before the bell rang; Jim hated bells.

He told me on several occasions as if I had forgotten or that he had overlooked telling me;

"The only two institutions in the United States with bells are prisons and schools. Now that should tell you something."

Jim went to his briefcase and withdrew his tape recorder, checked the batteries and checked the tape, turned sharply to his left, walked out of his room, and headed down the long hallway to the office. As he approached the outer office door, he clicked on his tape recorder, opened the door, and walked to Belinda's desk.

"Ms. Bookmann, Mr. O'Francis to see Mr. Bales as directed."

She smiled at Jim, got up, and went to Damon's office door.

"Mr. Bales, Mr. O'Francis is here to see you."

All Jim could hear was a grunt, and Belinda returned to the center of the office area and informed O'Francis to go in.

Jim walked into Bales's office and stood arm's length from the corner of his desk.

"Have a seat, Mr. O'Francis."

Jim did not respond. He took the first chair to his right, leaving one empty chair arm's length to his right.

Both chairs were dark brown with wooden frames, forming the chair's arms with medium brown leather seating and backing. Jim crossed his left leg over his right and placed his hands in his lap, cradling his tape recorder in his left hand.

Bales had not looked up at Jim as he wrote on a legal pad on his desk. A full minute went by before he looked up at O'Francis.

"Mr. O'Francis, I have two items I want to discuss with you. Your lesson plans for last week as well as this week. And you're partaking in dancing with students at school dances. Which I do not approve of, but...." Then he saw the tape recorder in Jim's hands. He pointed toward the recorder.

"You can turn that off."

"Well, in all due respect to your present position, Mr. Bales, that will not happen."

"Yes, I told you to turn THAT off. I don't mind you taking notes, but you will not use a tape recorder in our conversations."

"Well, Mr. Bales, if you prefer taking notes, I do not mind at all, but as for my choice of recording any of our conversations, it will be done via taping. Moreover, Sir, I believe we have had this conversation once before. Now, if you have nothing you would like to discuss with me that is noteworthy of recording, I have papers I need to grade, so if you will excuse me."

Jim stood, but before making his now-infamous military turn, which he knew irritated his principal, Bales commanded him to sit down.

"Fine. It has been reported to me that you and your wife have been dancing with the students at these, these, ahh, whatever they are, dances. What do you have to say about that?"

"Well, I would say that is a fact."

Damon looked at James O'Francis, thinking he would have denied the allegation.

"Okay, I forbid you or your wife from partaking in such activities or school functions. What kind of people are you anyway. Do I make myself clear?"

Jim smiled, "Oh yes, Sir, no more dancing."

"Now I want to address your lesson plans. They are unacceptable." Expecting a response from Jim, Bales paused.

Jim said nothing. He sat in his chair, legs crossed, hands in his lap, looking directly at Damon.

"Okay, if that is how you are going to be." Bales held the two sheets of paper up and directed them at Jim.

"I want to know why you are teaching about religion in your class. More significantly, these other religions!

"Just how is it that you think you are some expert on these things? Mr. O'Francis, I am tired of having parents call me and complain about your classroom lectures that these students do not need to know anything about. I really do not understand you. I do not have these problems with my other teachers. Why can't you follow the curriculum along with everyone else?"

Jim cleared his throat.

"Well, Mr. Bales, let me start by stating that I am following the curriculum."

Bales started to speak. Jim held his right hand up in the air with only his index finger extended upward. "Sir, if I may be allowed to continue without interruption." Bales' face began to turn rose-colored.

"Now, according to the text and the county curriculum, world geography encompasses all the world's major religions. Therefore, to better understand all these religions, I have provided them with factual information, maps, and charts as to their time of origin up to the present day. In addition, as part of the worldwide religious structure, I have included all the branches extending from the origin of the roots of each of the world's major religions.

"Now, as to the expert part. I have done extensive research on the subject matter and have had 15 hours of college courses on the subject. And I might add, from a highly reputable University.

"As to parents calling you, I do not understand why they would call you. I teach the course and can answer any of their questions concerning my teaching material. I will say that my students enjoy the subject matter and are somewhat interested in gaining knowledge. I have not had one complaint about any of the notes or material, in general, I have provided to them.

"The point of fact is, and in contradiction to your statement, they are asking many excellent, intelligent questions, and the subject matter has sparked great interest."

Bales' face had slowly changed from a very light rose to a dark blood red when Jim finished. His hands had curled into a fist as they rested on his desk.

Jim's voice remained calm and steady throughout the entire time he talked. Finally, he had finished his comments concerning his lesson plans. He calmly sat very erectly in his chair, and there was silence in the office for thirty seconds.

Jim never took his eyes off Bales. It was as if an eruption was building deep inside the very bowels of a human volcano. The magma rapidly made its way up through the vents, with a major eruption about to occur, blowing the very top off the "mountain."

Then like a volcano, he erupted, voice raised.

"Let me tell you something. I do not intend for you to continue on the same path you are going. Therefore, I will not allow you to teach any religion in your classroom other than the true religion, which is the only real religion in the world. Do I make myself clear on that matter?"

"I understand what you have said, Sir. However, the fact remains that there are other religions throughout the world. The course calls for introducing these other religions incorporated into the text. All I am doing is providing a more clear understanding of these religions. I am not teaching the theology of these religions but the historical facts about them. Unfortunately, the text does not do so, and as a teacher, I have to provide the students with as much knowledge about the curriculum's subject. The text leaves vague areas without explanation."

His voice was still normal and calm.

Bales stated, "I do not care about the world's other religions, and the parents in this area do not either. So now you will stop teaching about these religions at once."

"Does that include this religion you are referring to?"

Bales snapped back harshly and loudly.

"You just do not get it, do you? You are in the Holy of Holy Bible belt, Mr. O'Francis. This is not some school up north. If you want to tell the students about the true religion, I do not have a problem. But you are not to talk about any of the other religions."

"Well, okay, Mr. Bales. But you have not told me what religion I am to enlighten the students with?"

"What?" Bales yelled.

"Well, you stated the true religion of the area, correct? Well, Sir, just what religion is that?"

"Are you just totally incompetent?" His voice increased in volume.

"Sir, I am neither incompetent on the subject matter nor am I violating any school or state policy concerning the subject matter."

"Mr. O'Francis," as he drew out his last name, "Have you ever really read the "good book?"

"Mr. Bales, if you are referring to the "Book," which you all have dubbed the "Bible," yes, I have. I have found it fractured with many anomalies, a not so greatly written history book, and I might add, with one-hundred-and-fifty contradictions in the narratives presented within the pages of this "Holy Book."

"Did you say history book?" He stated with anger. His face was still blood red, the veins in his neck bulging, his face distorted with hatred as Bales leaned slightly forward.

"Yes, I did. It is very subjective, to say the very least."

"What?"

"Knowledge, Mr. Bales, is the most powerful weapon on earth. Something you and your kind fear more than death itself."

"You are a heretic," he screamed.

"Ahhh, yes, Mr. Bales, you are correct. That would be my choice to make."

"Do you not go to church?" He lashed out, not recognizing what O'Francis had just stated.

Jim sat saying not a word, knowing that Damon missed the meaning of heretic.

"Well, do you, Mr. O'Francis?"

Jim still did not respond.

"The protestant religion is the only religion, the true religion of the world. It is the only real Christian religion in the world. It is the only way to real salvation. It is the word of "God." I am a deacon in my church, and I am telling you that is the way it is going to be as long as I am the principal of this school. You will obey me, and you will not make any reference to any of these other so-called religions in your classroom."

Jim began a slow smile, which eventually crossed his entire face.

"Do you find this to be humorous, Mr. O'Francis?"

"Well, Sir, the point of fact is, I do."

At that, Bales stood, shoving his chair violently backward and slamming it against his rear wall.

"What are you anyway? Are you some kind of devil worshiper?"

"No, Mr. Bales, I am not. I was baptized Catholic in a Cathedral in Tulsa, Oklahoma. However, I question your devotion to this religion you are referring to."

"What?"

"I think you heard me correctly, Sir. I need not repeat myself."

"That explains a lot." As he stood red-faced and emboldening of himself.

"Which means what, Mr. Bales?"

Bales paused for a moment looking down at O'Francis as if he had made a statement that troubled him, then sat back in his chair heavily. He pulled himself back up to his desk, his facial expression strained. Then, picking up his pen, he wrote on his legal pad. Jim remained seated in his chair in silence. Finally, Bales put his pen down and leaned forward slightly onto his desk.

"Mr. O'Francis, I do not consider Catholic's Christians. You can believe what you like, of course, but you will not teach anything other than the facts about the Protestant religion in your class. It is what has saved this Nation, it is what this Nation believes in, and I will not have you corrupt these children's minds with false information, is that clear."

Before Jim could respond, Damon continued, "I think you have covered enough about religion in your class as it is. So move on to the next section. Whatever that is?" Then he looked down at his paper as if he was reading what he had written and then began to write again, picking up his pen.

"Mr. Bales, before I go, I would like to tell you that to teach about the origins of your Protestant religion, I had to incorporate the religion of Judaism and Catholicism and their origins. I did not mean to influence anyone's way of thinking; I simply wanted to present the students with basic facts about the different religions. I want them to learn to think, question, and seek knowledge."

Again Bales put his pen down and with his body gesture of disgust, slowly leaned back in his chair, took a deep breath.

"I do not know where you get all this insane information about the Protestant religion. You are wrong! Catholicism and Judaism, teaching them to think and gain knowledge, you apparently do not know what you are talking about! So now, you are not to teach any other religion in your class!"

Again, he leaned forward onto the top of his desk. His teeth were locked together as he spoke through them.

"Do I make myself clear Mr. O'Francis? Your teachings are insane!"

"Sir, insane?"

Damon's voice lowered, a first for Jim, his eyes looked dark, and his facial expression turned hard.

"That is correct, insane! You really do not know whom you are dealing with here. I know all about the Bible and am well aware of true religion. You are confused. You do not want to cross me."

His intimidating performance did not frighten Jim, and he began laughing.

"You have got to be kidding me. Mr. Bales, in all due respect to your current position, you are sadly misinformed. But moreover, as far as the roots of the Christian religion go, your religion or the one in which you sat in that chair at this present time and claim is your religion, and the one I was born into comes from Judaism. That is a fact. Facts are all I have ever dealt with.

"Since I do not have the time to educate you about Judaism and Catholicism, maybe you should join my class and learn about the roots of the religion you claim you believe in. Furthermore, since I have never been biased regarding any religion, you could also get educated on the fundamental beliefs of other religions worldwide.

"If you want to talk about who and what you worship, we could schedule an afternoon, and you and I can get down to the real issues. Evil."

Bales became so angered his hands began to tremble, his face became distorted again, and he looked as if his blood pressure was off the scale.

"I have heard enough of this blasphemy. You will not teach anything related to any religion in your class. I don't care if it is in the text or not. Skip it! I do not want to hear of you teaching anything related to religion! If I do, I am recommending your immediate dismissal. Now get out of here."

He waved his right arm foreword, flipped his hand as if to back slap some insect away, then looked down at his notepad, picked up his pen, and began writing quickly.

Jim stood, turned sharply, walked to the door, stopped, turned around, and took two steps back toward Bales' desk.

"Mr. Bales, to answer your question, I know exactly who you are. It is the people that are exposed to you that do not know. However, you, Sir, have no clue as to who you are dealing with. Good talk. We should do this again sometime. You have a blessed day."

Jim turned sharply and exited the office. He was but a few steps from Bales' office door when he heard him state, "Pagan!"

O'Francis smiled when Damon Bales uttered the word "Pagan."

Jim walked by Belinda's desk and wished her a good day, and thanked her, walking out of the office. Midway down the hall, he clicked off his tape recorder. Talking aloud to himself, "*Well, that went rather nicely. No more dancing, right? Gees...Damn, he really would have had a stroke if I had told him I included the history of Paganism and all of its connections to Christianity in my lectures.*" Then Jim laughed aloud.

The Abduction

Damon Bales had been a frequent visitor to the Cellar Llounge for many years. The lounge was located in the lower part of a very lavish hotel in the middle of Abetton, a historical town with lots of 1700 and 1800 buildings.

The timing was critical, and there had been many hours put in on surveillance to make sure the mission was completed without any hitches.

Damon and his wife arrived at 8:30 P.M. they went into the more Plush room off to the right of the dance floor, where live music was being played for the younger crowds that came to be entertained for a Friday night. The Plush room was more casual and relaxed with four luxurious oversized soft, beige colored, heavily padded chairs and two oversized soft padded couches. There were four modern hardwood square tables with four chairs and two smaller round tables with two chairs located about the room. A television was situated to the room's rear, usually carrying the news channel. A long bar was located to the left of the door as one enters the room with ten hard oak wood, soft padded seated bar stools with concaved backs, and a television in the center of the back and above the bar, usually carrying the sports channel.

As you entered the more popular forty by forty-foot entertainment room, there was a stage where the live bands would play. Just to the front of the stage was a dance area that could accommodate thirty to forty people. Just to the rear of the dance floor, there were ten tables with four chairs per table. To the far left side of the entertainment room, there was a separate room labeled the Rustic room, with a large opening with an old antique decor, eight tables with four chairs, and four with two chairs scattered about the room. Low lighting, A romantic atmosphere; thus, one could sit and enjoy the sounds and sights of the band and the people dancing. Still able to talk and be heard.

A fireplace was located at the very back of the room, usually lit with gas logs, and gave off a warm glow in the dimly lit room during the late fall and winter. To the right of the fireplace was an exit door with two steps leading out into the back of the hotel parking lot.

As one entered the Rustic room to the right, a short hallway led to the restrooms, the women's room was the first on the left as one went down the hallway, and the men's was at the far end of the corridor.

Brian O'Francis' Hawker Siddeley HS 125 arrived at Missoula, Montana, at 0600 hours, taxied to the hanger, and stopped.

James Patrick O'Francis waited until the plane stopped before getting out of his truck. He stood by the open truck door dressed in Wrangler blue jeans, a long-sleeved blue denim shirt, brown western boots, and a tanned leather coat with a sheep lining. The early morning fall Montana air was quite cool, and Jim had his winter gear on as the warm air exhaled from his lungs gave the temperature away.

As the plane's hatch was opened and the steps were lowered, Bruce Beck exited the plane and looked toward the few parking slots at the far end of the hanger. Then Bruce walked down the steps and toward O'Francis.

"Good morning, Jim. How are you this great morning?"

"I am doing well, Bruce. Good to see you."

"Are you ready?"

"Yes. Let me get my bag." Jim reached across the seat and picked up his small leather dark blue travel bag. He closed the door to the truck, clicked his electronic door lock twice, and walked with Bruce toward the plane.

The pilot revved the jet engines up, moving to the runway.

"I will get us some coffee as soon as we are airborne."

"Nice plane Bruce," Jim examined the light tan leather seats.

"Yes, it is. Brian has several. Not all like this one, but they all are fast and comfortable."

They were in the air and cruising at twenty thousand feet in minutes.

Nick Zileri was forty-five years old, with black hair with a touch of gray on the sides. He was six foot two and weighed two hundred pounds with dark tanned skin. Tony Mauriello was thirty-five years old with short dark brown hair, cut in a military-style, olive skin tone, stood six foot two, and weighed two hundred and twenty pounds. Finally, Joseph Scirrotta was the youngest of the three, 33 years old with a smooth Mediterranean complexion, black hair, six foot four, and two hundred and thirty solid muscular pounds.

They had arrived at the Cellar at 7:45 P.M. and had taken the last table next to the restroom hallway. Joseph would walk from the Rustic section of the Cellar nightclub to the less noisy Plush area and scan the room every ten minutes.

By 8:45 P.M., they knew that Damon Bales was present in the lounge. Damon usually only stayed at the Cellar for about two hours each time he came, twice a month.

At 9:30 P.M., Damon passed in front of the table where the three men sat and went down the hallway to the restroom. Nick rose from his seat first, and then Joseph and Tony. Nick took a position at the door, and Joseph and Tony went into the restroom.

Two other patrons were departing the restroom as Joseph and Tony went in. They quickly checked the room for anyone else and found that they were alone other than Damon. Tony stepped back out the door and told Nick.

Two minutes later, two other young men came down the hallway. As they approached the restroom door, Nick flashed a badge and informed them that there was a slight problem inside and could they give him a few minutes. The two young men stated that they had no problem with that and returned down the hallway.

Damon finished urinating and stepped to the sink to wash his hands; Joseph walked quickly over to him from his rear and placed a chloroform cloth over his nose and mouth with the force of a vice. Within moments Damon's body was as limp as a wet dishrag. Tony and Joseph lifted him placing his arms over their shoulders and came out the door. Nick led the way down the hall and to the right to the exit door.

The few patrons in the room at the time looked but said nothing. Most were dancing in the entertainment room to the loud music played by a local band.

They quickly carried him to the SUV parked close to the exit door. Nick opened the right back door, and Joseph and Tony shoved Damon into the back seat. Tony got into the passenger's seat, and Nick got into the driver's seat and started the SUV.

Three minutes later, they were out on the main street, headed to the signal light at the end of the street. They made a left, and two minutes later, they were entering the interstate headed south.

A thirty minute drive and they drive up to the private hangar where the private jet was already prepared to taxi out onto the runway for takeoff. Paul walked over to the SUV as the three men unloaded Damon and carried him onto the plane.

Nick smiled at Paul as he approached.

"It went like clockwork."

"I'll take care of the rental," Paul stated. "You all have a safe trip, oh, and tell Jim I said hello and that I will be in touch."

"Will do; later, Paul, and thanks for the help."

"Hey, not a problem, glad to be of service."

Within minutes, the plane was airborne, heading west.

Ten minutes had passed, Damon had not
returned, and his wife got up and approached the
manager Ted Mason, who was standing at the door
entrance to the lounge. They knew Mason, as they had
been regulars for several years.

"Mason, would you check on Damon as he went
to the restroom ten minutes ago and has not
returned?"

Mason informed her he would and walked to
the men's room. There were four other men in the
room, and he looked around, checked the stalls, and
found that Damon was not there. Mason came out of
the restroom and went back into the Rustic room,
scanned it for Damon, then stepped to the large
opening leading to the dance floor room and checked
it, and no Damon. He returned to the Plush room and
informed Mrs. Bales that Damon was nowhere to be
found and asked if he could have stepped out with
someone to the patio, which was to the rear of the
lounge by way of the exit door. She informed him that
she did not know but did not think so? Mason told her
he would check for her and did so.

He returned to inform her he was not there. A

sense of panic came over Evelyn Bales, and Mason could see it in her face. Mason called security, and they began a search for Damon. When he was not found, they started asking the patrons in the lounge if they had seen an older man anywhere and gave them the description and what he was wearing.

After forty-five minutes of inquiring, two couples sitting next to the fireplace informed the two security men that three men had helped an older man out the exit door. Asking about how long ago, they told the security men that it was about an hour earlier and that it appeared that he was passed out and that they were just helping him. None could describe the three men, as they had not thought about the matter.

At that point, Ted Mason called the police, and they had arrived at the Cellar in a matter of minutes. Evelyn went into a hysterical mode, claiming that something terrible had happened to him, and then began going on about a man named O'Francis.

The police questioned her in Mason's office and inquired who O'Francis was, and she informed them that he was Damon's sworn enemy and that he was very dangerous.

They had learned nothing while continuing the investigation throughout the rest of the night and into the morning hours. No one had seen anything nor heard anything. All they had was three men helping an older man out of the exit door.

Nick and company had arrived at the Hunt airport at 2:00 A.M. with a confused and scared Damon Bales. They loaded him in a Jeep Grand Cherokee, then took the route to the warehouse.

Bruce and Jim arrived at Hunt Airport in Portland, Texas, at 9:00 A.M. and got into a rental SUV. They drove the same route to the warehouse south, to Port Street, and went to the end of the street where they pulled up to a large warehouse, one of several "shell company buildings" owned by the Spadolini Corporation, at 11:00 A.M. Bales was sitting at the end of a long table in what appeared to be an empty warehouse.

The Long Table

Damon sat at the end of a ten-foot-long, five-foot-wide old dusty work table and had been told to keep his mouth shut.

The large warehouse was dark except for a Coleman lantern that burned opposite Damon at the far end of the table. There were no sounds to be heard other than the burning of the lantern. Damon was exhausted, his eyes were heavy from lack of sleep, and he would drift off from time to time and jerk himself awake only after a few minutes.

The faint light of the morning sun filtered through the breaks in the old broken windows high above from where Damon sat alone. The sunlight streams revealed the dust in the air as he looked around, trying to locate someone, and then he spoke.

"Who are you, and where am I?"

From a distance to Damon's rear, a deep voice replied.

"I suggest you sit in your chair and say nothing."

Damon did not respond for a few seconds, and he spoke again.

"I need to stand up."

Joseph appeared from the rear of where Damon was seated.

"You may stand."

Damon slowly rose. His legs were numb and stiff, and his buttock was sore from the hard wooden chair he had been sitting on. He turned slowly to face Joseph. Then, in a slow older man's sounding voice, he asked.

"Who are you, and where am I?"

Joseph stood ten feet away from Damon and did not respond to his question.

"Can I walk around?" Damon asked.

"Yes." Joseph stood erect, his hands cupped at his waist area, his feet shoulder-width apart. "You may walk around the table, and that is all."

Damon's insides quivered, and his skin became covered with bumps as he slowly walked around the table.

The warehouse floor was covered in very fine dirt, collecting for many years. The clean-up and new construction within a section of the enormous warehouse had begun.

The pigeons began their morning activity of flying in and out of the many openings high in the upper parts of the building.

As Damon circled the table, he looked around the vast space and saw nothing other than the man standing at the far end of the table. He could not see to the far end of the warehouse, some three-hundred feet away, because of the dark shadows. The sound of a door being opened was heard in the far distance to the rear of Damon.

Joseph spoke in a calm, deep voice, "You may take a seat now."

Damon stopped at the only chair at the table and stared at Joseph. Joseph never said a word, he just stared at Damon, and the look alone was all it took for Damon to obey his request. Fear reflected on his face and eyes as he finally took a seat.

Damon heard a vehicle enter the confines of the warehouse, the engine turned off, and then several doors closed. His heart began to beat faster, his skin became hot, and beads of sweat appeared on his forehead. He placed his hands on the dusty table, and then he lifted them and looked down at the dust on his hands. Then, slowly and softly wiping them on his dress slacks, he placed his hands on his lap.

To his rear, he could hear men's voices. Several minutes passed, and then there was silence. He looked around from side to side, but he did not turn and look to his rear.

It was as if an eidolon had manifested at the end of the long gray-white dust-covered table. The lowly flickering lamp gave off a shadowy figure of a man; his head was tilted downward; he had a large flat-brimmed dark brown western-style hat on, and the brim was slightly bent down in the front and back.

His thick full extended white mustache was trailing down to the bottom edge of his lower lip. The man stood motionless for several minutes. Silence permeated the large warehouse. Damon sat staring at the person opposite him.

Slowly, the man reached his left hand up, removed his hat, and placed it on the end of the dusty table. His head was still tilted downward. Damon could see he had gray-white hair, slightly long covering his ears, trailing to the back of his neck, parted in the middle, and the hair and mustache matched in color. But unfortunately, Damon could not see the man's face because of the lack of illumination.

The man stood motionless and silent for several minutes. Then slowly, the man looked up and directly at Damon. Finally, the illuminating light from the lantern revealed the man's face. At that moment, he saw his face and took a deep gasping breath as if he was looking directly at an apparition. Then he stated,
"YOU!"

The response was, "Time has come today."

O'Francis raised his right hand, holding a black cylinder magnum Smith & Wesson .357. The man pointed the pistol directly at Damon, and then squeezed the trigger. The bullet struck Bales in the center of his forehead, sending his body backward over the chair and onto the dusty warehouse floor, spraying a smattering of dust upward. The echoing sound reverberated throughout the building sending the pigeons and other birds fluttering and flying about in the upper part of the large empty area.

Moments passed, and O'Francis stood motionless, his arms at his side, his pistol in his hand. He slowly reached down and picked up his hat, placed it on his head, and calmly walked to the far end of the table where Bales lay. The chair lying on its back, Damon's arms lay outward from his lifeless body. Pieces of his skull and brains lay a few feet from his head. Blood was soaked up by the thin layer of dust on the floor, turning it an even darker color red.

O'Francis looked down at Damon, then, without a word, placed the pistol in his should hostler, walked to the awaiting vehicle, and got into the passenger side's back seat.

Minutes later, a woman and a man appeared with a robot the size of a six-foot man. It was being remotely controlled by the woman. She nicknamed it "PAD."

Headline News

John O'Donovan got up at his regular time of 7:00 A.M., showered, got dressed, went to the kitchen, and put on a pot of coffee. He then went down to the garage, clicked open the garage door, drove down the mountain to his paper box, retrieved his Monday morning paper, and returned to his home at the top of the mountain.

The morning mountain air was a bit cool, in the mid-40s, with a slight breeze, which made it feel like it was in the 30s.

John went back into the kitchen, got his oversized coffee cup, filled it, and went into his great room to his favorite chair, placed his cup on the rustic pine table to the left of the chair, and sat down. The chair faced the east side of the great room, which had a solid glass window from the ceiling to the floor. There was no deck outside, which allowed him to view the forest and its creatures without obstruction.

The great room was on the second floor, allowing him and Boaz to look down and over the cleared land some twenty yards to the edge of the tree line. He enjoyed just sitting and looking out at the forest and, on occasion, deer that would graze on the soft grass between the tree line and his home.

As he got comfortable and ready to read his paper, his cat "Boaz" jumped into his lap for his morning petting session. "Boaz" had shown up at John's home some five years earlier and had taken up residence with John. John enjoyed his company; he took him to the vet, got him the proper shots, and neutered him. "Boaz" was a rather large black and white cat with three white paws. John had no idea what kind he was but had become very attached to him.

He administered his morning petting as "Boaz" purred in his lap as they sat and looked out the window while John took a sip of coffee from time to time. Then suddenly, "Boaz" jumped down and strolled over to his hand-built bed/chair/perch at the base of the entire window to observe what was happening below him if anything.

John reached over, picked up his paper, and scanned the front page.

"Well, now let's see what has been taking place over the weekend, "Boaz," as if his cat understood him. "Boaz" looked over at him and gave a soft meow in response to John's statement. He then looked back out the window and laid down, folded his front paws inward, and settled on his perch for the morning.

John looked over the front page, quickly reading a few articles and scanning as he usually did. Like most of the time, nothing interested him. However, on this day, one article did catch his attention. On the right side was the heading, Damon Bales missing.

He read the article and quickly got up, went to the kitchen for more coffee, and went to his den for his file on Bales. It was ten o'clock as John re-entered the great room, and the phone rang. He picked the cordless phone up and walked to his seat.

"Hello, John O'Donovan here."

"Morning John, its Anthony Krause. How are you this fine Monday morning?"

"I am doing well; how about you?"

"I am fine. Say, I have some questions for you. Have you read the paper today?"

"Yes. Why?"

"Well, have you read the article on Damon Bales yet?"

"Yes. I found it interesting."

Anthony proceeded to tell him that he just so happened to be present at the Cellar Friday night when he had disappeared in front of everyone and that no one knew who had abducted him. Anthony followed the investigation and hoped John could tell him a little about the man and his wife's accusation that O'Francis had something to do with his disappearance.

"Well, Anthony, to tell you the truth, I have not seen O'Francis in several years, and I really do not know where he went. However, I seriously doubt that he had anything to do with Damon's disappearance. By the way, where were you when all this took place?"

"I was in the Plush Room where Damon and his wife were. Several of us guys had a night out together, and just out of nowhere, there were police all over the place asking everyone all kinds of questions. His wife went off the chart. The paramedics had to be called in and had to take her to the hospital as she was having heart palpitations, and they thought she was going to stroke out on them."

"Well, Anthony, sounds as if you had an exciting evening."

"Yea, unexpected, but the right place at the right time. John, did he and O'Francis have some problems back in the earlier nineties?"

"Yes, but my God, he had problems with many people. Just because his wife stated that O'Francis would have had anything to do with his disappearance is a stretch, I would think?"

"I don't know, John. She seems to think that Bales constantly fears he will do something to him. And it is the only name that seems to be coming up."

"Well, what have you turned up? What have the police found out? Also, Anthony, if someone is so fearful as you say Bales' wife stated, what did Bales do to create this fear? So what you are telling me, you have no leads?"

"Nothing, absolutely nothing. I think the local police have turned it over to the F.B.I. They are treating it like a missing person's case. No one even knows O'Francis. They have been over to Honsburg to see if anyone knew where he had moved and found nothing. They went by the county school system, and I guess all the people there were relativity new and had heard of him but did not know where he was.

"Well, I followed up on the school leaders, but no one knew anything. But, hell, retirees have to get a check, don't they?"

"I would assume so."

"Isn't that part of the VRS?"

"I really don't know, Anthony."

"It is as if he just disappeared from the face of the earth. That is what makes this even more intriguing. So, can you help me out here?"

"Tell me, Anthony, have you been to Honsburg yet?"

"Oh yes, but the people there do not know where he went."

"Have you talked to the town police yet?"

"Yelp, did that too. However, after O'Francis' son and his wife's death, the Chief told me that O'Francis left about seven years ago for parts unknown. I even tracked down and talked to the retired police chief. By the way, John, wasn't O'Francis and the retired Chief over there good friends?"

"Yes, to the best of my knowledge, they were."

"Well, do you think he was telling me the truth about where O'Francis could have gone?"

"Yes, I would say he was. I think James O'Francis just up and left without telling anyone where he was going. Actually, he was more of a recluse than anyone realized. So, I don't think he told anyone why or where he was going."

"Well, tell me this, John, did he not give you any idea of where he would have gone? I mean, you and O'Francis got tight, right?"

"Well, I would say we were well acquainted. I would not say that we were tight, as you put it. Jim just walked off one evening, and I never heard from him again. So I tried locating him, even went by where he lived, and he had sold his home, cannot remember the young couple's names. So I asked them, but they did not know. They said they had gone through a local realtor. And before you ask Anthony, yes, I went by the realtor's office and spoke to the person who sold the home for him, and they knew nothing."

John sat in his chair and smiled as Anthony continued to probe in hopes that he might get a lead on James Patrick O'Francis' whereabouts for a big news story.

After a fifteen-minute conversation of which, Anthony had gotten no new information. He asked John one question before bidding John goodbye.

"John, do you have any idea as to what a black lily means?"

John paused in conversation. "No, I don't think I do. Why?"

"Well, the police found one lying on the restroom sink at the Cellar. I just thought it might have some significance?"

"Well, I really cannot help you there, Anthony."

Then, he requested that John contact him if he could think of or if he happened to come across anything of importance or newsworthy, from one semi-retired reporter to one working a case.

Investigation

Captain Bushman stepped to his office door and called detectives Branch and Bass into his office.

"Yes, Sir."

"I have been looking over your notes on this Brewer case. I think there is more to the case than meets the eye. I want you to go to Honsburg and do some investigating. I want to know what the connection is between the other cases. I have been on the phone with the Chief in Liberty, Jefferson City, and Abetton. They will provide us with all the information they have on their cases. I want you to find out all you can on this, ahh..." He turned over the two pages of notes on his desk, "ahh, O'Francis. I want to know if there is any connection. His name has cropped up several times, according to these other police departments. Find him."

"Okay. But...we have been over it with several people, including the Reynolds County Sheriff's Department, and really they had very little to help us. Captain, no one knows where this guy is."

"Do it again. Somebody may remember something. Talk to the locals; find something we can go on. There is just something about this that is nagging at me. I think there may be something to that phone call."

The two detectives left the office and headed for Reynolds County.

They arrived in Honsburg at 11:00 A.M., and as they approached the town's post office, they pulled into the parking lot, thinking that the postmaster knew everyone in a small town and would be able to give them at least a lead on O'Francis.

Burt had a blue sports coat, white shirt, red tie, tan slacks, and brown loafers. Jason had a tan jacket, light blue shirt, dark blue tie, tan slacks, and brown loafers.

They approached the counter inside the post office and requested to see the Post Master. In a few seconds, Mr. Jon Waldon, a Marine, came to the counter.

"May I help you?"

"Yes, you may," Burt said.

"I am Detective Bass, and this is Detective Branch. We are from Kinstown. Is there someplace we can talk to you privately?"

"Yes, in my office. It is that door over there," as Jon pointed to the far side of the room. "I will open it for you." Jon opened the door in a few seconds, and the two detectives stepped into Waldon's office.

"Gentlemen, how may I help you? Have a seat." Jon pointed to two chairs in front of his desk. Jon's office was rather plain, with a few pictures of postal history on the wall but nothing else. His desk was clear of any paperwork. He had a stapler, tape dispenser, and one penholder on his desk with three pens.

"We are investigating the death of one of your county residences, a Dunkin Brewer. Did you know him?"

"I knew of him."

"You did know he was found dead in our area a while back, didn't you?"

"Yes, read about it in the paper."

"How about a Richard Finkel?"

"Yes, heard about that one also, but did not know him."

Bass paused for a few seconds thinking the Post Master would continue with the conversation, but Jon sat in his chair, waiting on the next question.

"Okay. Mr..." Bass paused as he forgot the Post Masters name.

Jon answered, "Waldon."

"Yes. Sorry, Mr. Waldon."

"It's okay."

"Okay, what about a woman by the name of Janice Jones. Do you know her?"

"Yes. I knew her. I have not seen her in many years. I think she moved away. Ahh, maybe up in northern Virginia; not sure about that part, but that was the gossip in town."

"Well, actually, Mr. Waldon, she is on a missing person's list. She disappeared about six months ago from the town of Liberty. So the FBI is looking into that.

"Oh, I was not aware of that," Jon said.

"Well, that is okay. We are looking into the possible connections between these people since they all seem to be from this area."

"Branch spoke for the first time in the conversation." He opened his notepad and looked at it.

"Do you know a man named Damon Bales?"

"Yes, I knew of him. He was a principal here at the high school for a time back in the, ahh, let me think...I think maybe in the 1980s. Not really sure about that. I was not around here back then. The Corp had me."

Jason smiled, as he was also part of the Corp. Then stated, "Once always, correct?"

"Jon quickly stated, "Correct, Simper Fi."

"Okay, Jon, were you aware he is also a missing person?"

"No, I was not aware of that either. So I am assuming that the FBI is looking into that one also?"

"Yes, they are, as well as us."

"Well, how about a man by the name of O'Francis? Did you know him?"

"Yes."

"Know where we can find him?"

"No."

"Know anyone who might?"

"Well, O'Francis used to live around here, but he moved several years ago. I really don't know where. He never left any forwarding address for us. He just up and left after he lost his wife."

The two detectives continued to ask Jon Waldon questions about the missing or dead people, figuring that being a small town, he would know. They asked him about the police chief and were informed that he probably would not know much. He is young. Jon told them of the retired police chief and told them where he lived stating he might be able to help them.

After discovering that Jon's wife, Rachel, also knew O'Francis, they got directions to her workplace, the local elementary school where she was a secretary.

After asking Rachel many questions and getting no new helpful information, they checked with the town police chief, who gave them nothing as he had not known any of the people.

However, learning that Mr. Charles Headley Winslow, the owner of the local hardware store, might know, as he had been around a long time. So the two detectives stopped by the local hardware. They gathered information on all the people on their list. However, none of it seemed to get them any closer to finding the whereabouts of Mr. O'Francis. So they headed to the retired police chief's house, who lived several miles away, on a backcountry road.

Running the back roads and getting lost twice, they found former Chief Higgenbottom. After thirty minutes of probing, they ended up with no more than they had when they left Honsburg.

After returning to the office and reporting what they had not found to Captain Bushman, their report did not go well. Captain Bushman sat looking at the two detectives. "What? This man just vanished? Is he dead? What? I mean, I don't think people can disappear."

Jason spoke, "Captain, I don't know about that. I mean, some people do just that. They do not want to be found. They become total recluses."

Captain Bushman's only comment was, "Hmmm."

Legs

There had been questions by the newly elected school board concerning monies not accounted for. But no one seemed to get any real straight answers. La Mar had for years been funneling large sums of money into an unknown account, using various means and personnel, primarily his loyal bookkeeper and lover. But the time had come when too many questions were being asked, and the newly elected school board was discussing legal charges, a school board in which he had only two members he could control and would support him, leaving four that would probe deeper and expose him for what he was— a thief.

Such a legal undertaking would be lengthy and costly. So instead, the school board members bought his contract out, and he walked away with a sizeable chunk of money.

La Mar moved on to the newer and better "ground," east, to the far end of Virginia, where he would begin a new career as a school system superintendent that did not know what they were getting. Unfortunately for the school system, La Mar Marshy had been hired; he continued his corrupt actions of hiding money and shifting it around, skimming off bits and pieces into his now lucrative offshore account. Given all the years of practice in Reynolds County, he was an expert at it.

When he left Reynolds County, he hung everyone remotely connected to him out to dry, including his lover and bookkeeper, who lost her job but without jail time for her part in the alleged embezzlement that no one wanted to pursue in a court of law.

Bruce was once again clicking roll after roll of film of Marshy when he left his home to his arrival at his new school's central office to his social events to his extra-marital affairs, which he continued with his newfound lady at his new school district.

Bruce had logged his travel times to and from various places and had plotted a drafted plan of action for Marshy's abduction. O'Francis was not involved in the kidnapping, but in "Time," he would bring the mission to its justified end.

Bruce and Paul had met with Brian in St. Louis at one of Brian's hotels. They had discussed the mission in every detail and were putting the final touches on it. Once again, Jordan was involved as Marshy's weakness was attractive women.

La Mar Marshy had trimmed his weight from two hundred seventy pounds to a more present appealing two hundred pounds. Jordan and Bruce arrived in Richmond via Brian's private jet, and Paul arrived via car, picked the team up, and checked into the Holiday Inn Airport on Williamsburg Road.

Having dinner and reviewing the final plans for the pick-up of Marshy, they retired for the evening. By 0600 on Friday morning, they were on the road headed west, weaving their way through the city of Richmond on Route 60 and into the countryside to the small town of Buckingham.

Jordan Black used her alias for this mission as Felice Eugena. She had made an appointment with Marshy two weeks in advance; she represented a private computer software company that wanted to test their new math and science software on real students before releasing it to the public. It was at no cost to the school district, and the school district would be allowed to keep the new software. Marshy agreed to talk to her and gave Ms. Felice Eugena an appointment for 10:30 A.M.

Jordan walked into the central office at 10:15 A.M.

"Ms. Felice Eugena to see Mr. Marshy. I have an appointment at 10:30."

At 10:30 on the dot, Marshy walked out into the lobby of the central office. Jordan was sitting with her left leg crossed over her right, and Marshy almost gave himself away by taking in a gasping breath when his eyes gazed upon the stunning beauty of Jordan. Her smooth dark Native American legs were exposed up to the middle of her thigh, and his eyes flashed instantly to them. And Jordan watched his eyes as he approached and knew she had him. She was dressed in a black sleeveless body-fitting top-of-the-knee dress that outlined her hourglass body shape, with black high-heeled open-toed shoes. She stood as he approached, and Marshy's eyes gave themselves away once again as they traveled the entire length of her body.

She stuck her hand out, "Mr. Marshy, I am Felice Eugena. Thank you for seeing me."

The Marshy smile went from ear to ear. "No, thank you for coming." Then he held his hand out, indicating for her to go through the door to the far right of the receptionist.

As she went by him, her very expensive perfume penetrated La Mar's nostrils sending "goose bumps" down the middle of his back. His predator instincts activated instantaneously.

They retired to his office, where she gave him her pitch and presented him with the artificial portfolio. As Jordan handed La Mar the portfolio, she shifted her legs several times from left to right and left as she reviewed each page of the software company's offering. Jordan watched his eyes, and each time she shifted her legs, La Mar looked up from the portfolio and looked at her. Finally, after a forty-five-minute conversation about what the software company was willing to do for his school district, Jordan made her move. "Mr. Marshy..."

He interrupted her, "You can call me La Mar."

"Okay, La Mar, as I was saying, it has been a rather long trip from Texas, and I wondered if there is a place one can stay overnight as my flight back does not leave until late Saturday evening."

Marshy informed her where she might stay and instantly lost his train of thought as his mind went to half of a night in bed with her.

"Mr. Marshy, is there anywhere one can go to lunch in your town?"

"Oh yes, there is a lovely restaurant five minutes from here.

"Would you like to join me for a bit of lunch? It will be on the company, and we can continue our conversation over lunch, as I am a little hungry. I came straight from the airport, and I have not had anything to eat."

Marshy gladly accepted the invitation, and they walked out of his office. As he passed his secretary, he informed her he was going out to lunch and would be back by one o'clock. As they exited the central office building, "Felice" told La Mar they could take her car and promised she would not kidnap such a hunk of a man. Marshy laughed loudly. "Felice, being kidnapped by you might be interesting."

"Yes, La Mar, I think it would." She smiled and made eye contact with him.

He agreed to take Felice's car as they walked toward a black Chrysler 300. The sides and back of the car windows were darkened, and Marshy could not see the two men sitting inside the front seat as they approached the car from the rear. Paul and Bruce watched them through the side mirrors as they walked twenty-five yards from the front door of the central office across the parking lot. Being the gentleman he was, he walked Jordan to the driver's side as she clicked the key chain to unlock the doors. As he opened the driver's side door, Jordan stood beside the left rear door, talking and smiling, keeping La Mar's total attention.

"La Mar, you are such a southern gentleman. I did not know that existed in this century." Felice's words prompted La Mar to turn his head to the right and look at "Felice" for an instant.

"Why..." is as far as he got. At that moment, Bruce wheeled out from under the steering wheel and sent a breath-exhausting blow to La Mar's mid-section, bending him over. Marshy only saw an instant blur of a figure emerging from the car.

Bruce grabbed his suit coat at the right upper shoulder and presented a pistol in his face, and a low deep voice ordered him to get into the back seat as Jordan had opened the left rear door just as Bruce struck him.

La Mar was still gasping for air to refill his lungs and could not respond as Bruce forcefully moved him into the back seat and got in beside him, closing the door behind him.

Jordan got in the driver's seat and closed the door. Paul had reached over and started the engine just as Bruce had struck Marshy. Jordan backed out of the parking spot, shifted to drive, and headed for the parking lot exit. The entire sequence of events had taken place in less than a minute. There had not been anyone leaving or coming during this minute. As they exited the parking lot, a FedEx truck and a car entered, but they could not see into the car's side windows, so they had no idea who was in the car. Marshy was still trying to get his breathing back to normal as he laid his head back and sucked in the air. His mid-section ached with pain.

"What are you doing?" he finally gasped out.

"Kidnapping you." As Bruce leaned over and softly spoke into his left ear, Marshy's eyes were fully dilated as he slowly looked over and gazed into the dark brown, almost black, cold, hard eyes of Bruce Beck.

In two days, the "great" La Mar Marshy would come face to face with the man at the end of the long table. Then, as fear engulfed his face, he would hear the words, "**There is no time limit**." And then the last words he would ever hear, "**Time is up**."

Impending Danger

Jim's contact with the DEA was done covertly. He used an alias and mailed the information he had gathered to the only honest State Trooper he knew, Lenny Vaga.

Jim had gone downtown to obtain material from the hardware store for his summer home improvement project.

O'Francis exited Winslow's hardware store, walked the few steps to his pick-up truck, and opened the door. He looked down the street to the corner. Standing at the intersection were two former students and a man he did not know.

Bobby Joe looked toward O'Francis. Jim closed his truck door and walked the half block to the corner.

Bobby Joe had been a favorite of his when in school. He encouraged him to get off the pills and cut down on his use of marijuana each time he saw him. O'Francis did not walk away or shun him when they passed on the street or when he crossed paths in one of the stores in the town. O'Francis was not totally opposed to the "Mary Jane" if one partook of it in moderation.

Bobby had always liked O'Francis because he was one of the very few teachers in Honsburg High that had helped him and pushed him so he could graduate. Bobby knew that he would have never graduated if it were not for Jim's guidance. Bobby knew that O'Francis did not like the street business he was in, but he always spoke and asked how he was doing. He knew that he always had something positive to say before they parted.

Jim approached the group and spoke to Bobby first.

"What's up, Bobby?"

"Ahhhh, nothing much, Coach." Jim looked at Darrell and spoke.

"How you doing, Darrell."

"Okay, Coach. How are you?" Jim smiled at the two former students as he spoke to them.

"Ahhh, I am doing well, I guess, same ole same ole, you know how this school system is run."

As both nodded their heads yes, they spoke in unison. "Oh, yes, we know."

Jim then addressed Bobby Joe.

"So, what are you doing nowadays, Bobby?"

"Ahh, working as a flagman on that construction job next to Liberty."

"Well, good. Do you like it?"

"Well, yeah, I guess. It's a job, Coach."

"Well, you never know; if you stick with it, you may get a chance to move to something better, working for a large company like that. I know one of the owners of that company, as we grew up together. If you like, I will speak with him." Then Jim looked at Darrell.

"So, Darrell, what are you doing with yourself?"

"Nothing. Just hanging out."

"No job?"

"Nope."

"Well, did you check with the construction company that Bobby is working for? They may need something done. Or at least they will have your application on file."

O'Francis' peripheral vision caught the front expression on the man's face of what Jim figured to be a thirty-year-old. Jim did not know the man and did not bother to introduce himself nor ask his name. It may be a small-town operation, but O'Francis had been in the presence of a more significant operation. He knew and felt the environment he was currently in.

When Jim started to ask Darrell another question, the man with a thick full black beard, black hair down to his shoulders, faded-out jeans, and a jean jacket tattered at the ends of the sleeves spoke in a rather deep voice.

"Sure do ask a lot of questions, Mister." O'Francis did not look at him or comment on his statement.

"Darrell, you need help getting a job someplace, a reference maybe?"

When Darrell answered O'Francis, his tone had changed slightly to a harsher one.

"No, man, I don't need anything." Jim smiled as he spoke.

"Well, if you ever do, just let me know. If I can, I will help. Okay." Darrell never answered O'Francis.

O'Francis patted Bobby on his left shoulder.

"Bobby, you need anything? You know where I live."

Bobby smiled at O'Francis. "Okay, Coach, I will. Thanks, Coach."

"Hey, no problem, be glad to help. See you two guys. Do good now, you hear." Bobby was the only one who replied, "Okay, Coach."

Jim turned and walked back to his truck. He looked in his driver's side mirror and saw the bearded man looking at him as he approached his truck. Jim got in, turned the truck around, and drove by the corner, waving at the two young mid-twenty-year-olds as he paused and took another look at the bearded man.

At 10:30 that night, the phone rang at the O'Francis house. Patrick answered, and Jim heard him coming down the hall to the den.

"Dad, it is for you."

"Who is it?"

"Don't know? It's a man calling from a payphone."

"Okay, thanks." He pivoted in his swivel chair and reached for the phone.

"Hello."

"Coach. It's Bobby."

"Well...Bobby, my man. What can I do for you?"

"Coach, I really need to talk to you."

"Okay. I am all ears."

"No, coach, not on the phone."

Jim paused, knowing it was not for advice from his former teacher.

"Okay. When would you like to talk?"

"Coach, I know it's late, but could you meet me tonight?"

O'Francis' thoughts were that it was very series by the tone of his voice.

"Okay. Ahhh, where are you now, Bobby?" Jim could hear people talking in the background and the sounds of automobiles. Bobby cleared his throat.

"I am at the Exxon now. I know it's late, Coach, but can you meet me down on Lewis creek?"

"Okay, Bobby. I can handle that. Where?"

"How 'bout where the road turns up from the river? You know where that white church is?"

"Yes. Give me twenty minutes."

"Coach, it's really important."

"Bobby, I'll be there. I promise. Have I ever made a promise I did not keep?"

"Nope, not to me."

"Right. Then I will be there in twenty minutes."

"I'll be there, Coach. See you in twenty."

Then he hung the phone up. Jim waited for several seconds listening before he placed the receiver down.

As Jim put on his western boots, Dawn came down the hallway and into the bedroom.

"Who was that?"

"An ex-student."

"Who?"

"Bobby Lebert."

"What did he want?"

"He needs to talk to me about something."

Jim went to the nightstand on his side of the bed. He opened the top drawer and removed a .357 Smith & Wesson. Then he took out his shoulder holster and put it over his Notre Dame tee shirt. He took the cloth off the revolver, opened the cylinder, checked the shells, and positioned the cylinder where the first shell would be the quarter shot shell fired. Every other shell was a .357 hollow point. Dawn did not like what James P. was readying himself for.

"What is going on?"

"Don't know? He just wants to meet me and talk about something important."

Dawn's voice expressed concern.

"Don't worry. I'll be careful." He kissed Dawn and went out the back door grabbing his Levi jacket off the coat rack as he went out.

He traveled the dirt road following the creek until it emptied into the river, then followed the dirt road that ran alongside the river, passing one house after another, some with lights on, some with no lights. He arrived at the church within twenty minutes. He pulled up beside the driver's side of the dark blue 1987 Chevy Cavalier with gray primer paint on the left front fender and the right quarter panel. He turned the lights off. It was very dark, with no streetlights in the area. Jim's eyes adjusted quickly to the dark. He then turned off the engine. He rolled down the window.

"Hello, Bobby. Fancy meeting you here." He said with an optimistic tone. James P. knew it was no time for jokes.

"Hi, Coach. Sorry for the late-night call."

"Ahhh, it's okay. So, I assume this is important, for such a covert meeting?"

The look on Bobby's face told Jim that he did not know what the word covert meant. Jim told him.

Jim opened his door and stepped out. Bobby opened his door and got out. O'Francis noted that his dome light did not come on in his car.

"Okay, Bobby, let's talk over on the steps." So the two walked fifty feet to the church steps. They sat on the second of the five steps that led to the church doors.

It was a cool night, fifty degrees. Bobby took out a pack of cigarettes and lit one. Jim pulled a cigar out of the inside pocket of his jacket. He reached into his right outside pocket, took out a cigar cutter, clipped the end off, and licked the cigar from one end to another. Put the cutter back into the pocket, took out his lighter, and lit his cigar.

"Coach, I know you know I smoke pot, and you don't tell nobody. I know you don't like drugs."

Jim said nothing for several minutes. He just let Bobby talk as he puffed on his cigar.

"Bobby, one thing about "pot," I never said I did not like it. I do not have a problem with people using

"Pot," if used correctly. Been there and done that. For your information. Okay. Now, other forms of drugs I do have a problem with it. Again, for your information."

"You know that guy that was with Darrell and me today."

Jim looked at Bobby in the dark of the night.

"Didn't know him."

"Well, he's a dealer. He wants me to work for him. He wants me to push the hard stuff for him. Said he would pay me well."

"Uh-huh," Jim uttered.

"But that is not what I want to talk to you about." O'Francis did not say anything. There were a few moments of silence as Bobby gathered his thoughts.

"Look, coach, he knows you are trying to stop the drugs in Honsburg."

"Hmm. I see," Jim responded.

"Coach, you know that cops are working for the county that are working for the drug pushers in the county?"

"I see," was all the response that Jim gave.

"They know about you, Coach."

"Okay. So, they know. Bobby, I make no secret about my efforts to stop the drug traffic in Honsburg and the county."

"I know. But…" then Bobby stopped talking. There was a long silence, and all that could be heard was the river flowing some fifty yards in the distance, just over the embankment. Then Jim spoke.

"But what, Bobby…hell man, don't stop now. You wanted to talk to me. Shit, man, just come out with it."

"Okay… I was told that they are going to put a stop to you. That you cost them too much."

"How?"

"I don't know. I guess by telling somebody about the drug deals in Honsburg. You know that several people have gone to jail."

"Yes, but not the ones that should be in jail. It is the users, not the dealers! People like you, Bobby. I do not want you users. I want the dealers. I want the money man or men, whichever the case may be! I want the people at the top. And for the record, Bobby, I know a few deeply involved people, and they are at the top, your good upstanding church-going citizens. That is who I want the legal system to nail."

"Well, that is what I mean. The cops are involved. They are on the take. And they are the ones that are telling on you."

"Well, Bobby, how do the cops know I am passing information to the DEA about the drug dealers?"

"I don't know. I know that they have been talking about you."

"Well, tell me, Bobby, who are they?"

Bobby had put out his cigarette and lit another. Jim sat quietly, arms resting on his knees, taking a puff off his cigar once every minute or so.

"Coach, this is really serious. I mean, these people are really bad. I mean, you can't tell nobody we are talking."

"Bobby. You do not have to worry about that. I give you my word that no one, I mean no one, will know we talked."

"I mean..." then he stopped. He took a deep drag off his cigarette and flipped the ashes off the end. He took the same position as O'Francis, looking out into the dark of the night.

He finished his second cigarette, dropped it at his feet, lifted his left foot, and crushed it out. Jim held his cigar between his left index finger and middle finger. He touched the half-inch of ashes at the end of his cigar to his left knee, and the ash dropped at his feet. Put the cigar to his mouth and puffed on it a few times.

"I mean what, Bobby?"

"Well, there is some talk that they are, ahh, they are going to take you out."

Jim never moved, he did not talk, just looked out toward the river. The night carried the sound of the water rolling across the rocky shallows of the river as it turned and followed the mountain ridge as it had done for thousands of years. An owl pierced the silence of the night.

"I really don't know the main man. I know the two-county cops are working with the people I know."

"Who's the guy on the street with you today?"

"That would be Jake Salvador. Or that is what I know him as."

"So, where is he from?"

"Don't know."

"Who's the cops?"

"Sam Crouse, Greg Felton, Danny Vachel, and John Lakeland."

"Anybody else."

"Not sure. I don't think so, could be. Hell, Coach, I think the Sheriff is in on the deals."

"So how "they" supposed to do me in?" "Don't know? Just that some of the guys been talking about it. You know some of the guys don't like you, Coach."

"Yeah, well...I'm not too fond of some of them either. Works both ways, Bobby." Then again, there was silence for several minutes.

"Know who is supposed to do me?"

"Nope."

"So, who told you that somebody would do me in?"

"Got it from James and Ted. They don't like you. Said they hoped somebody did."

"Where did they get the info?"

"They didn't say. Just said they had heard."

"James and Ted have any dealings with the cops."

"Yeah."

"How you know that?"

"They told me."

"Why?"

"Why what?"

"Why did they tell you?"

"I don't know. Just was talking one night. They said they wouldn't bust them if they worked with them. So Lakeland and Vachel met with the dealers."

"How you know that?"

"Hey, Coach, we see things. We know who is doing the deals and who is getting the money. Ahh, once in a while, they get us some free stuff. You know how it is."

Jim did not comment on Bobby's statement.

"So, who does the most contact with the dealers?"

"Lakeland and Vachel, for sure. Not sure about the others."

Jim's cigar was three-quarters of the way smoked. He reached the cigar between his feet and touched the long ashes to the concrete steps; it broke off smoothly. He straightened his back, arching his shoulders back, and several spinal desks popped.

"Well, Bobby, this is really interesting. Got anything else for me?"

"Nope. Just that."

"You think they, whoever they might be, are serious?"

"Yeah, Coach. I mean, Jake is one of them, I think."

"One of the ones going to get rid of me?"

"I think so."

"So, Bobby, why you telling me?"

"Cause I like you. I know you don't like what I do, but I am trying to stop. You know, cut back. I don't like all this talk about getting rid of you. You helped me when I was in school and all. I think you should know. I mean, you might be able to, you know, stop them or something."

"Uh-huh. I see. Well, maybe." Jim stood. "Tell you what, Bobby, let's call it a night. You let me know if you get anything new on getting rid of me, okay?"

"Okay, Coach, I will." Jim shook his hand and thanked him for the warning. They got in their vehicles and departed.

Winners and Losers

Patrick was not as fortunate as his older brother when it came to his high school days. Patrick's class was generally made up of losers, people who were drug users and would, in time, become dealers and movers of the "cancer" that beleaguered the community in which Patrick lived and grew up, a place where Jim had moved to escape the blights of the big cities of America.

However, the "cancer" that gripped all cities, large and small, in its death grip had spread to the small towns and rural communities.

Dawn and Jim worked hard to stay on top of Patrick and his attitude toward academics, which started back in his junior high school days.

Like most, if not all, public school systems throughout the United States, either because of unions or just the fact that the administrators were incompetent to do the jobs, making sure the students got a good education and weeding out the deadwood, non-caring, incompetent teachers.

Teachers like Fred had done more damage to students and their overall attitudes toward learning than any the O'Francis' had ever seen. Unfortunately, Patrick was one of his victims, and it was up to his parents to try and correct the damage. The administration at the school was deplorable, with little or no leadership, not that it had been all that good over the years the O'Francis family had lived in the community. The high school's negative environment carried over into the community.

Nevertheless, Dawn and Jim had kept a positive attitude about Patrick's career, pushing him to excel and overcome the negative he was exposed to daily.

Patrick's high school days ended with a bitter taste in his mouth, both athletically and academically.

He went to college but did not desire to excel at a higher educational level. He maintained a 3.3 GPA. Although his intelligence level was there, his will was not. Two years later, he dropped out to work in the oil and gas drilling profession.

The students who had skimmed by in high school had graduated to the street, where they made more money selling and dealing in the drug world than Patrick did in his profession as a driller and with much less physical labor.

Patrick's use of marijuana was recreational and on weekends. Jim had mixed feelings about "MJ." He knew it was no worse a substance-abusing product than that of alcohol or, for that matter, as he would tell me, cigarettes. In some cases, less of a problem for society as a whole. On the other hand, he knew it was classified as a drug because of the religious-political powers controlling the elected legislators of which he also knew the legislators catered. Regarding the O'Francis parents, the hypocrisy was so entrenched in the political spectrum that you had no integrity if you were a politician. Jim worried because "MJ" was currently illegal, jeopardizing his son.

Turning Point

It was another typical teenage and post-graduation teen party, and Patrick was in attendance, like many of his high school days. Beer and marijuana were the main courses for the night. In addition, there were pills of assorted highs, and the ever-present coke provided by the more affluent filtered through the ones who could pay for it. The ages ran from seventeen to twenty-six, with a social-economic class ranging from the poor to the wealthy side of town who had gathered for a night of alcohol, drugs, and sex. When it came to class distention, wealth, race, gender, or intelligence did not factor in the end game.

As it was BYO, Patrick chose his favorite, Crown Royal. It was one-thirty in the morning when the drug task force rolled in on the house, grabbing one after another, slinging them to the floor, and striking them with their batons.

Anyone with long hair, boy or girl, clothed or naked, was grabbed and pulled or slung against a wall or onto the floor. One would have thought by how the local police officers were conducting themselves that it was 1968 and the protest riots instead of 1998 and a drug bust on a group of youths.

The Reynolds County Police had slept through the class on police abuse. So the Reynolds County drug task force was putting on an impressive show for the State drug enforcement agency that was present.

Patrick had never been a violent person, a little on the passive side unless pushed, and then his Irish surfaced. He was clean-shaven with a military haircut. However, he was no angel. But he was a young man living life, learning its pitfalls as he experienced the era's norms. Nor were any present "little angels" gender irrelevant, as seen in most parents' eyes. All gathered that evening were arrested and dragged out of the house. Some were just drunk, some were high, and some were both.

Patrick raised his arms high in the air to the approaching county deputy.

"Hey man, I am going, no problem," he stated clearly to the county deputy. But that was not enough. He could not grab his hair, so he took his baton and struck him behind his knees, sending the six foot two, two hundred pounds Patrick to the floor. Then, using his black Gestapo-style boots, the deputy's foot caved in Patrick's left rib cage, then a blow to the right side of his head with his baton, bringing forth a gush of blood. Just as the deputy struck Patrick with his baton, a state trooper walked into the room.

"What the hell are you doing?" he yelled in a deep voice.

"Teaching this piece of shit a lesson!" replied the deputy in his toughest, tough cop tone.

The Trooper stepped between the deputy and Patrick. Then, reaching down, he assisted Patrick to his feet. Even with the blood covering his head and the side of his face, he recognized who it was.

"Holy shit!" The Trooper exclaimed. Then he helped Patrick to a county police car and told him to stand by the door and not move. The County deputy watched as the Trooper walked away. Then he walked toward Patrick, stopped, and looked at him. Patrick's head was lowered, his right hand over the gash on the side of his head, blood dripping between his fingers to the ground.

"Yeah, I know who you are, too! I never liked your piece of shit "old" man anyway! Fuck him, too!" he stated with bitterness in his voice. Then with a quick, violent motion, his right elbow caught Patrick's left jaw, sending him to the ground, putting Patrick's mind in a semi unconscious state. He took his right foot and drove it into his face, breaking his nose and gashing open his lips.

Trooper Vaga had been talking to two of the States' drug agents and had looked toward the squad car where he had placed Patrick just as Crouse's foot made contact with Patrick's face.

He instantly broke into a run toward Crouse from some thirty feet away, with his large hands grabbing the deputy by his coat and slinging him away from Patrick to the far side of the squad car. Vaga's structure was much larger than Crouse's and had no problem handling him to the vehicle's far side.

"You know, you are one stupid son of a bitch! You know who that boy is?" he yelled at the county deputy. Trooper Vaga's face was inches from Deputy Crouse's face, the brim of his hat touching Crouse's forehead like the old days of a military D.I. With a smirk on his face and a sarcastic tone to his voice, Crouse replied, "Yeah, I know who the little son of a bitch is! So, what makes him so god damn special!" Deputy Crouse snapped back.

Trooper Lenny Franklin Vaga, L.F. for the

people who knew him, had known James Patrick for over forty years, and Jim had provided Vaga with information that had led to several rather large drug busts throughout the county. Vaga was part of the State Drug Task Force and only two in that part of the state with German Shepherd drug dogs.

To Trooper Vaga, Jim was one of the "good guys" and a good friend. Vaga knew Jim's background, knew he had worked under William Peng and was trained by him in martial arts and police procedures.

Anybody in law enforcement in the entire state knew if you worked for and had been trained by William Peng, you had to be a clean Law Enforcement Officer. Vaga also knew of James Patrick's elite military background. Vaga himself was a veteran of the Viet Nam Conflict and, like Peng, had served the Marine Corp with pride and honor.

As he had his "man to man" with Deputy Crouse, Lt. Samuel Drake, the Reynolds County Officer running the drug task force, seeing the conflict between the two men, approached the scene.

"L.F., what the hell is going on?" he asked.

"One of your finest here has most likely cost us one of our best supporters and a valued link to information we normally cannot get!"

Lieutenant Drake had a look of puzzlement on his face. Vaga saw it.

"Follow me!" he stated harshly, his voice strong and filled with anger, with both hands holding onto Deputy Crouse's coat. Vaga shoved him hard against the squad car, stating,

"Stupid! Just plain damn stupid!" Vaga walked Lieutenant Drake around the car where Patrick lay on the ground, still dazed. Vaga squatted and helped Patrick set up, telling him who he was as he leaned Patrick against the car's back door. Samuel squatted and shone his light on his now cut and bloodied face.

"God damn it!" Drake yelled out. "Well, Fuck! I don't believe this shit!" He continued his colorful metaphors. He stood, took two steps away, turned, and looked back at Patrick, "God damn it!" Then, taking his hat off and slamming it to the ground, yelling at the top of his voice, "Crouse!

Crouse had mingled with the other corrupt deputies that riddled the County Police Department. He did not hear Drake yell for him as he was bitching about how Patrick O'Francis was being treated differently from the others they had arrested.

"I don't know why Drake likes O'Francis so god damn much. Hell, I think he is a piece of shit!" Deputy Brent Whitt spoke, "Well, I'll tell you why," as his face became crimson and his voice denoted his anger, "The same fucking reason I like him! He was our teacher and coach. He was a damn good one—the only one who really gave a rat's ass about others and me in high school. Now Crouse, I really don't know why you don't like Coach O'Francis, but some of us do. I have heard enough. So, just keep your fuckin' comments to your fuckin' self."

"I can't stand the son of a bitch! Hell, Brent, you know god damn well where he is when it comes to our, and by god, that includes you, side job! So, why should you give a fuck about O'Francis?"

Then he paused. None of the other four deputies was saying anything. Then Crouse continued.

"Hell, man, he would hang your ass just as quick as any of the others we deal with, and you know it."

At that point, "Big" Jamie "Red" Flennor walked over to the group. He was one of only a few that had not caved into the temptation of the extra money from the dealer.

Jamie Flennor was better known as "Big Red," standing six foot six and weighing three hundred pounds. His strength appeared to be beyond human.

Jim had taught his daughter and son in school and had worked with "Big Red" when there was no corruption in the County Police Department under William Peng.

"What is this I hear about Patrick O'Francis being hurt?" he asked the group. Crouse knew that Flennor also liked O'Francis. However, he did not like Flennor and spoke,

"Yeah. He's over there," as he pointed toward Trooper Vaga and Drake. Drake called out Crouse's name the second time. "CROUSE!"

Flennor looked at Deputy Crouse.

"Drake wants you," Flennor stated as both deputies walked over to where Drake and Vaga were.

Flennor walked to the side of Vaga.

"What's this about Jim's son Patrick? I didn't see him when we went in the house."

"Come with me," Vaga stated. Drake and Crouse walked off in the opposite direction.

Patrick had lain down on the ground against the back wheel of the squad car, in pain, inside and out. His mind numb from the experience of being brutally beaten by one of several corrupt Reynold County cops. Vaga and Flennor walked to where he was. Jamie squatted down, placed his mage light on the ground, and like a giant grizzly bear, gently raised Patrick and leaned him against the back wheel. Vaga shined his light onto Patrick's face.

"Oh my God. We need to get him to the hospital L.F., like now! Shit. Who did this?" As the gentle giant rose to tower over his longtime friend, Lenny Vaga, who was a huge man himself,

"One of Drake's boys!" Lenny stated.

"Who?" Jamie asked.

"Crouse. I saw him hit him twice. I don't know how many more times. Bastard. You know "Big Red" what this means." Neither one spoke. They just looked at each other and shook their heads. Then, Jamie stated, "Yea, I know."

"I know we had better get Patrick to the hospital. I damn sure know that. Damn, Lenny, he is hurt bad."

"Help me get him in your car. You can go ahead and take him. You tell Drake."

Trooper Vaga squatted down to assist Patrick up. Patrick was still dazed and felt the total pain of his bruised ribs and busted-up face. His legs were like rubber as Flennor and Vaga carried Patrick to Vaga's State Police Car.

The Phone Call

It was 3:30 A.M. when the phone startled Jim awake, a parent's greatest fear— a phone call in the middle of the night.

"Jim, Coach," the unrecognized voice on the other end of the line said.

"Yes, speaking," O'Francis said, his heart pounding harder each second.

"Samuel Drake here. Sorry to bother you at this hour of the morning, but you need to come over to the jail."

Jim sat up in the bed, becoming instantly awake. Being awakened by the phone, Dawn felt his sudden movement and raised.

"What's wrong?" she said with the fear of a mother's voice. Jim remained calm. "Brother Drake," as both belonged to the same Masonic Lodge, "What is it?"

"Well, it"s Patrick," Samuel stated.

"What?" Jim replied.

"Jim, he was at the wrong place at the wrong time tonight. He is okay, just a small problem. Look, I will handle it. Just get dressed and come over to my office. I'll be upstairs, okay?" Samuel stated firmly.

The twenty-minute drive seemed to take longer than twenty minutes. Maybe it was because he and Dawn rode in silence the entire way.

As they climbed the wooden stairs to Samuel Drake's office, their footsteps seemed to echo louder than usual in the old narrow wooden stairwell. He opened Samuel's office door at the top of the stairs and was met by Samuel with a cup of coffee in his hand. He handed it to O'Francis.

"How about you, Mrs. O'Francis?" he asked. Trooper Vaga was seated to the left of the door entrance and rose, all six foot four and two hundred thirty pounds, extended his hand, greeting James P. in his deep voice,

"Morning Jim, sorry about this. Mrs. O'Francis." as he nodded at Dawn.

"Okay, gentlemen, where is Patrick?" Jim asked. Samuel answered,

"Jim, he is at the hospital." Samuel glanced at Dawn. "Now look, Mrs. O'Francis," as the look on her face told them everything, "He'll be alright."

James P. looked around the room before he spoke. Lenny Vaga was still standing, Samuel was to Dawn's left, and Officer Watts, a plain clothes and sometimes undercover officer for a regional drug task force, was sitting to the far right-hand corner as you entered the room.

"Well, this must be really bad. Both of you are out tonight."

Then he turned and looked at Watts, "And you. You're part of this. So let's have it." James P. stated in a military tone of voice.

O'Francis was not expecting what he heard. Both he and Dawn had taken a seat as Samuel and Lenny explained what had gone down. There was a moment of silence after all had been said. Lenny looked over at Jim.

"We are not going to charge Patrick with anything. Our undercover man told us he was only drinking and stated that he had brought his own bottle of Crown to the party. Continuing, he had stated that he had not seen him doing any of the drugs. He was a little high but not drunk."

More silence as O'Francis took all that was being said as he ran it through his mind. He looked at Watts. "You there?" asked Jim.

"No," came the first response he had made since the O'Francis' had entered the room.

"We had someone their age working. He has been working undercover for some time now. He is a good man," Brad Watts stated.

"Jim," L.F. continued, "He was just at the wrong party at the wrong time."

Samuel spoke, "Look, I will take care of the overreaction by my officer. I truly want to apologize for all this. It is wrong, and I will take care of it. Please let me handle it, okay?"

O'Francis never said a word, just sat looking at Samuel, L.F., and Brad.

The phone rang. Brad picked it up, and by the conversation, Jim and Dawn knew that their son was down at the jail. He hung the phone up and turned in his chair.

"Mr. and Mrs. O'Francis, you can pick up Patrick and take him home now."

Lenny Vaga stood, and as Jim and Dawn stood, Vaga placed his large hand on his long-time friend's shoulder.

"He'll be all right. I'll talk to you in a few days. Jim, let us handle this. I promise you it will be handled properly. I promise."

As Dawn went out the door, Jim followed, stopped at the top of the stairs, and looked at Samuel. Samuel Drake stepped close to Jim, placed his hand on Jim's back, and whispered,

"Brother to Brother, I will take care of this. Take Patrick home, and care for him."

Jim thanked Lenny and Samuel, then giving Samuel a Masonic handshake, stepped back to the doorway, and shook Vaga's hand. He looked over at Officer Watts, pointed his index finger at him, and gave him a thumbs up. He and Dawn went down to their son and departed.

It had been three months since the incident had occurred with Patrick. When O'Francis was exiting David's grocery, Deputy Crouse was entering. He had been suspended for one month without pay and removed from the drug task force and was more bitter than ever at O'Francis.

The County Sheriff was retiring at the end of the year, and Sam Drake would run for the High Sheriff and get elected. He would, in time, change the image of the department and would, with time, get rid of the corrupt officers within the department.

Trooper Vaga would leave the State Police Drug Task Force after the loss of having his dog killed. He would retire because of politics and corruption within the State Police.

Jim waited on Crouse outside the store, and as Crouse exited, O'Francis spoke,

"Deputy Crouse."

He turned to face O'Francis.

"I just wanted you to know that there is no time limit," Jim O'Francis stated with a smile on his face.

"Just what does that mean?" Crouse puffed up in a manly posture as if he was about to exert his police powers on James Patrick O'Francis.

"Just what I said," O'Francis stated. Waved and smiled, "You have a most wonderful day, Mr. Crouse." Then James O'Francis turned and went to his car. As he drove off, he vowed to himself, no more police help.

A Pleasant Encounter

O'Francis had been working in his new job as the High School County Homebound instructor for several years and had become attached to it, as he found that he could achieve a great deal with students one on one. For the students on the higher intellectual level, he did not have to help a lot. Still, he enjoyed talking to them as they became more comfortable with each other and expanded into areas and topics that were taboo in the classroom.

For the students that did need a lot of help with whatever subject, Jim enjoyed passing on knowledge and was able to get them through the courses and raise their GPA. In addition, he was able to see the joy on their faces when they got their tests back with high grades than the grades for any given six weeks. It also made for delighted parents.

He also learned about teachers in the other three high schools in the county. Some were very good. However, a percent were terrible but could maintain their jobs, doing significant damage to select students; a concern for Jim when it came to homebound students was that certain students were treated differently than others, which led to more than one confrontation with specific teachers. However, with the aid of excellent record-keeping by O'Francis, the principals' support, and the additional backing of a newly appointed superintendent, "LT," as Jim O'Francis referred to her, O'Francis never lost a single "battle," and the students he had on HB won, which was all that mattered to O'Francis.

As the years passed so very quickly, he found that two of his former students had entered the field of IT.

They had gotten a job working for Reynolds County as the county was attempting to move forward into the world of high tech; not that anyone in control really wanted to, as none really understood the world of computers, and it would mean that the county would have to put forth more money to educate the student body. Not to exclude that, they would have to hire people who actually knew what they were doing in high tech. It was a matter of necessity that anyone on the school board approved any budget remotely connected to the field of IT. Reynolds County and the "know it alls" entered into the IT world as slow as the state and federal subsidizing would allow. Never leading in anything, but rather being forced to obtain materials and personnel to maintain the needed equipment to operate in a world of computers.

Jim was a forward-thinking individual, always thinking out of the preverbal box, and enjoyed conversing and associating with people who also did.

Upon arriving at his office at 0900 hours and having no students scheduled for that morning, he wandered into the IT department. But much to his surprise, when he ventured into the large area set aside for the IT department, he recognized two former students, brilliant and years ahead of the grade Jim had them in: Nobel Bryan and Blake Vanpelt. They were repairing computers and operating some individual school computer main servers that ran through their department.

Upon seeing their former teacher, all work stopped for a cup of fresh coffee and a long break. The conversation went from how they got there and had it been that long to a general "bitch" session about the lack of intelligence of the higher echelon that ran the school system.

O'Francis would, over time, learn that both were extremely gifted in what they did and were way above the level of intelligence of the people that did the hiring for the system as a whole. So every chance he could, which was not often due to his schedule, James Patrick would pop in on them and spend a little time talking to Noble and Blake. It seemed to lift his sometimes unpleasant day to a higher level when he could spend a few minutes with both, as they were positive, progressive thinking young men.

It also did his "soul" good to see his former students succeed. And, of course, a few good laughs when they would remind him of something that had happened in their class or something that he had told them and that they had never forgotten. Of course, Jim marveled at the "things" he did not remember taking place that they did. However, he did appreciate that they did not forget "O'Francis' Think Tank," the nickname of his room, and the answer to the questions, "What is the most powerful weapon on earth? And what is the worst thing a person can waste?"

The one thing I learned about O'Francis and his relationship with any one of his students was that it would last far into the future, and they would carry with them more than he would have ever thought they had learned.

The Hit

At three A.M., an SUV pulled into the parking lot of the Honsburg Fire Department. Since the mountain town's fire department was made up of volunteers, no one was on duty at the fire station.

The driver of the SUV turned off the engine and sat in the semi-dark of the parking lot, observing the houses leading into the Haldeman section of the town. He remained in his vehicle for ten minutes. No automobiles came into or exited during this period. Finally, the driver opened the door. The dome light did not come on. He stepped out, opened the back driver's side door, and retrieved a 12-gage modified 18 inches Winchester, model 700 pump shotgun. Quietly closing the back door and then the driver's door. Standing motionless for several minutes, he jacked one shell into the chamber.

He wore black ankle-high soft sole shoes, black leather pants, a black turtle neck sweater, a full-length black leather coat, black leather gloves, and black leather flat-brimmed western hat. He opened the left side of his coat and slid the shotgun barrel down into the special pocket sewn into the coat. He walked across the parking lot and onto Hickman Street, where he continued walking toward his assignment.

In a few minutes, he came to the first intersection, Hickman and Maple, where he veered onto Maple. He continued on Maple until he came to Pine and Maple, where he turned onto Pine Street. The streetlights were far enough apart that he became a shadowy figure as he made his way to his destination, the corner house. The night was cold, 28 degrees in the late month of February.

The weather report had called for light snow flurries. The night sky was dark with clouds, and a very light mist had begun to fall. There was no natural illumination, and the night seemed darker than usual. There were no dogs barking, no sound at all. A deathly silence appeared to cover the northwestern section of the town.

He stopped at 1700 Pine Street, entered the driveway, and then to the yard's far corner, where an eight-foot privacy fence separated the two houses. Directly across Pine Street at 1701 was the home of David "Country" Higgenbottom.

He stood in the dark corner of the yard, observing the one-level ranch-style home. The yard was sixty feet from the house to the street, with a row of pine trees along the Maple Street side and the one-hundred-foot front lawn up the Pine Street side.

A three-layered split rail fence lined the pine trees side of the yard, on the yard's edge ending at the driveway.

An open driveway and a short section of split rails continued thirty feet to the corner of the privacy fence. The privacy fence continued across the north side of the yard, separating the house at 1702.

The ranch-style home was an unusually long house for the area, some eighty feet. The house's front door was just off to the right of the driveway, with a five-by-twenty-foot deck from the entrance to the corner of the house. Then to the right of the front door was a bay window, then two-bedroom windows, a deck four feet off the ground started six feet from the second bedroom window. Finally, a large glass door allowed entrance from the master bedroom to the front deck.

It was now 3:30 A.M., and he walked to the back of the house by the privacy fence. The backdoor of the house opened onto a one-hundred-year-old handmade brick patio.

The outer door was a full glass wooden framed storm door. The man dressed in all black tried opening it; it was not locked. The inner door was a solid wood door, and he turned the knob slowly. It, too, was unlocked. He slowly opened it and looked carefully into the room as the man slowly stepped into a laundry room—typically with a washer and dryer. The room was eight by ten with shelves lining the walls with various food items and a pantry.

Another door, located in the middle of the wall directly opposite the outside entrance, was closed, but as he slowly turned the knob, he found it not locked. He gently turned the knob and opened it slowly. As he opened the door, it squeaked. He stood motionless for several minutes as he peered into a large room, the O'Francis entertainment room.

Then he reached into his right coat pocket and removed a set of night vision goggles. He removed his hat with his right hand, placed the goggles over his head, and adjusted them to his face. He replaced his hat, and then he scanned the room he was about to enter. At the far end of the room was a bar. Behind the bar, the wall to the front side of the house, was two small windows head high off the floor. A bumper pool table was in the middle of the twenty by fifteen-foot room.

The master bedroom was located at the far end of the house. The bedroom was large, thirty by twenty. A den, a walk-in closet, and the master bedroom's private bath were off the bedroom.

A set of double solid cherry wood doors separated the closet from the bedroom. A small eight-by-eight room separated the bath from the closet.

That room led to a den fourteen feet long and ten feet wide. The queen size bed was at the south end of the room, with a large window over the bed. Located in front of the glass wall, facing the front desk, was a vanity table with a flower arrangement on it. At the end of the bed, there was a short couch the width of the bed. To the right of the entrance to the master bedroom was a full wall entertainment center. Several of O'Francis' drawings lined the walls of the bedroom.

The bedroom door was open. James Patrick abruptly opened his eyes. He had been sleeping on his back; he heard the squeak of the laundry room door.

His youngest son Patrick had left at 11:30 with his girlfriend and had informed his parents that he would be spending the night with her.

Michael was in his final year of service in the military and stationed in Maryland, working at the NSA headquarters. Typically, if one of the sons came into the house late at night, the first thing they did was whistle. The family had come up with a unique whistle to identify each other when entering their home or locate each other when separated in a large store.

James Patrick's hearing intensified greatly at night, something he could never understand but welcomed the sense as a gift.

Even though his house was kept warm at a steady 70 degrees by the heat pump, he became cold. He and Dawn slept in the nude under a sheet, with a light cover and a bedspread if needed.

Dawn was soundly sleeping as usual with the security of her soulmate to protect her. She was on her right side, her back to Jim. He gently touched her on the shoulder; she was startled awake with an "Ahh, what?" Jim leaned over to her left ear and whispered,

"I do not want you to say a word. Just listen."

She turned her head and looked at her husband in the darkness of the room, trying to adjust her eyes. He put his left index finger over her mouth.

"I want you to slide out of bed on my side quietly, get on the floor, and get as much of your body under the bed as you can."

She did, and Jim put several pillows over her.

"Say nothing!" he whispered as she became scared. Her body began to tremble, and tears gathered in her eyes. She did what her husband told her.

Jim's Smith and Wesson .357 hung in its shoulder holster on the large bedpost. James Patrick also had his military .45 lying on his nightstand at his disposal. Full mag, and one in the chamber.

Stepping into the large entertainment room, the intruder located the door leading from the game room to the kitchen, and he stepped into the kitchen. He scanned the room, then turned right and passed through the door that led into the living room.

He stopped and looked about the room. He
faced the bay window side of the house. To his right
was a long couch; in the middle of the room was a
hand-carved wooden oriental coffee table. Across the
room, in front of the window, was a recliner. The
wall to his left was an entertainment center and then
a long hallway leading to the back of the house. He
looked down at the floor, hardwood. He walked
around the center of the room, passing by the coffee
table, and stopped at the hallway entrance.

Jim had slid out of bed onto the floor. He
reached down to his side of the bed to the floor, pulled
two oversized pillows up, and placed one on each side
of the bed, pulling the covers over them. After quickly
arranging the pillows to appear as if someone was
under the covers, he dropped to his knees and
stretched out to the end of the left side of the couch
facing the bedroom door.

The heat pump kicks on. Then, just as it did,
James Patrick cocked the hammer back on the pistol.
Several years earlier, while working with police officer

Chris Whitley, he had the trigger adjusted to a hair touch.

The room was pitch-black; he could not see anything, not even the white dots on the front and rear sights. As usual, the Roman shades had been let down, preventing any light from the outside from penetrating their bedroom at night.

Jim lay in the prone position, pointing his pistol at the master bedroom door entrance.

The intruder looked down the long hallway. He could see the far end of the hall and the door that entered the master bedroom. As he took his first step into the hallway, the floor squeaked. He stopped.

Jim had laid the hardwood floor himself and had made the wood give and squeak if someone stepped on it, another security measure for him. So at the end of the hallway, three steps before entering the master bedroom, the floor was designed to give slightly and squeak.

Slowly the intruder put his foot down on the floor with no sound. He moved slowly, one step at a time, pausing with each step. He stopped at the first room, the central bathroom. He looked to his left and scanned the room, then a few steps and scanned Patrick's bedroom to the left. Then the O'Francis library. The next room was the guest bedroom. The night vision goggles made everything appear pale green. Ten feet of the hallway were left before he reached the master bedroom door. Step, then he pauses, step, pause, step pause, and then a squeak as he placed his right foot down on the floor. He stopped. Peering through the bedroom door, he could only see a fourth of the room.

Jim's heart began to pound in his ears. Dawn had pulled one of the pillows over her head, exposing only the right half of her body. O'Francis held the pistol in his right hand, his left cupped under his right. His left thumb crossed the back of his right thumb. He was trying hard to see through the door. His eyes had adjusted to the dark, but he could not see anything. James Patrick's aim was chest high to what he perceived to be the center of the door.

The intruder pulled the shotgun to his right shoulder, then stepped without a sound. He stepped again, a slight squeak on the wooden floor. He paused. He was one step away from entering the bedroom. He could see the bed and two large mounds on the bed in a ghostly pale-like shape at the far end of the twenty-foot-long room. He heard nothing. He stepped into the room onto the thick tan carpet and fired once at the left side of the bed.

The red flame exiting from the end of the shotgun barrel told Jim what he needed. He raised the pistol barrel slightly and fired two quick shots just as the assassin jacked another round into the chamber.

James Patrick's first shot was the 1/4 ounce shell that hit the man in the face. The second was the hollow point .357, hitting the man in his upper chest and cutting across the right lung through his left back. The second shot sent the man back into the hallway and onto the floor. As he fell backward, he dropped the shotgun. James P. heard it hit the floor in the hallway. He was up and moved quickly to the handmade entertainment center on the right side of the bedroom door.

There he paused. He had to adjust his eyes again as the flash from the shots fired left white spots in his vision. He heard no movement, no sound. He stood with his back against the entertainment center, his arms folded up at the elbows and against his chest, the pistol pointing upward. He took a deep breath. Then, in one smooth, quick motion, he pivoted on his left foot, crossed the right over, and moved across in front of the bedroom door, pointing the pistol down at the floor and firing two more shots. First the ¼ ounce, then the .357 hollow point. James P. continued across to the double doors leading into Dawn's large walk-in closet.

He pressed his back against the double doors and waited. His arms were in the same position as before; his cross-over in front of the bedroom door had placed him only two feet from the bedroom door entrance. He heard no sound.

Dawn had buried her face in her hands. She was crying without any sound, and her body trembled uncontrollably.

Jim took his left hand off the pistol and reached his left to the doorknob of the closet right door. He turned the knob and swung the door open without a sound. He slid to his left and into the closet.

Then he stepped back to the wall, taking the standing ready position, his gun pointing forward. He reached the wall and flipped on the closet light—still silence. Quickly swinging outward, pointing his pistol toward the bedroom door, the light pierced the bedroom and illuminated down the hallway. He then slid the two feet of space between the closet and the bedroom doors and paused. Pistol pointing forward, he edged to the door facing; quickly, he looked to his right, down the hallway taking a mental picture of the hallway and then back. He had seen a body lying on the floor a foot from the bedroom. Again, he repeated the move, the same scene. He then looked around the door opening without withdrawing. He stepped out into the hall, standing at the feet of the body lying in his hallway, pointing his pistol at the man, the hammer cocked, he stepped to the man's left as he occupied the right side of the hallway. The shotgun lay at the intruder's right knee on the floor. The assassin's left arm stretched out over his head, his right arm to his side. His head lay to his right, the night-vision goggles still over his eyes.

Jim eased by the lifeless body and around to the top of his head. Holding his pistol in his right hand, pointing it at the man's head, he reached down with his left hand and placed his index and middle finger on the side of his neck. There was no pulse.

James P. then moved back to the dead man's side, reached down, picked up the shotgun by the stock, and laid it on the bedroom floor. He then quickly went to his wife's side.

"Dawn, it's Jim. It's okay, come out." She slowly rose out from under her protected covering. She grabbed her husband and hugged him tightly, breaking down and sobbing aloud.

"What the hell is going on?" she stated as she cried.

"Get dressed. I'll call the police."

Jim went to the phone on the nightstand, called "Country" first and told him he needed him to come over.

David knew that he did not call him over just for a bull-shit conversation, that this had to be an emergency. James Patrick then put on his jeans and Notre Dame sweatshirt lying on the couch at the end of the bed. "Country" entered the front door when Jim got off the phone with the county police.

He knew that the state police and the county would be at his home in ten minutes. Dawn was in the kitchen trying to get control of herself and putting on a pot of coffee, still with trembling hands. As "Country" entered the O'Francis house, he called out,

"O'Francis, what's up?"

"Dawn is in the kitchen," O'Francis yelled from his bedroom. "I'll be there in a second."

"Maw," as David had always referred to Dawn, walked into the kitchen to see his surrogate mother in emotional shambles, which did not sit well with him.

James P. went to the kitchen. Dawn tried to tell David what had happened, her voice still trembling, tears still filling her eyes and running down her face— shaken from the events that had just occurred. James Patrick walked in and looked at David.

"Come with me." They walked to the hallway, and he flipped on the light. "Country" squatted down and removed the goggles from the man's face. Small pellet shots dotted the right side of the man's face.

"You know him?" Jim asked.

"No. Do you?"

"No. Someone put a hit on my family and me, "Country!"

"What the hell is going on, Jim?" David rose to face his longtime friend, teacher, and coach.

"I really do not know. But I intend on finding out."

Dave squatted down again, examining the dead man's chest. "Hit him twice."

"No, four times." Dave turned his head and looked up at Jim.

"Pellets from the shot shells got him in the face twice. Hollow points got him in the upper chest and through the heart."

"Country," being the chief of police for many years in the town of Honsburg, rolled the body over to see his back.

Two large holes in his back indicated the exit of the hollow point shells. One had cut his upper spine. The other came out just below the shoulder bone.

"Country" rolled him back. He looked up at the wall in the hall, then raised and reached over and rubbed his fingers over a hole in the beige-colored paneling.

"First shot went through the middle of his back, probable severing his spine."

Jim looked at "Country,"

"You'll find the next shot in the floor under him." Then he proceeded to explain how it went down.

The County and State police arrived, and David Higgenbottom let them into O'Francis' home and explained what had taken place.

James P. stayed in the kitchen with Dawn drinking coffee. Of the four-county deputies and the two-state police that arrived on the scene, three were Masonic Brothers and former students.

The rest of the night was long, with lots of talking. No one seemed to know who the man was. No one understood why he was trying to kill James Patrick and his wife Dawn.

O'Francis knew but said nothing. He knew he would be getting a visit from the 29th District Drug

Task Force in the next few days. James P. had
questioned some of the people connected to the task
force but had no hard evidence to link anyone to any
of the top drug pushers in the area.

Paul O'Neill

Two days after the attempt on Jim and Dawn, he called O'Neill. It was arranged for Jim to meet him at his office. The following morning, he and Dawn were at Paul's office. Dawn sat with Mary J. in the outer office while Jim drank coffee and gave Paul all the details of the events that had taken place. Paul sat in his old squeaky wooden office chair listening to every word. When Jim was finished, he got up and went to the coffee pot, poured another cup, and held the pot toward Paul.

"Yes, please." Jim walked to the desk, refilled Paul's cup, returned it to the Bunn holder, put the pot back, returned to his semi-comfortable office chair, and sat.

"Jim, this is big. You have struck a major nerve. This is not a small town move."

"Yes, I am well aware of that. The question is, who? I mean..." then he stopped and took a drink of coffee.

"I do not think I did all that much to curtail the flow of drugs into the area. I mean, hell, Paul, a street dealer here and there, a few users, nothing to the real money people. What the hell?"

"What the hell, Jim, is that you have gotten someone's attention. That someone is afraid that your little one-person crusade against the flow of drugs will expose whomever because that street person you have identified will talk too much and surface their name. Jim, it may seem like little money, but it is not. The money is big. We are not talking a few thousand dollars here. We are talking hundreds of thousands of dollars. The kind of money that leads to someone in Miami, New York, places like that."

"Damn, Paul, I really do not." Paul cut him off.

"Jim, no offense here; you are yourself street smart. But, when the money trail goes up, it gets big. You cost these people some big dollars. And again, more important than the money, which they can absorb, is names."

They sat and looked at each other for several minutes without speaking. Paul continued.

"Someone in your little neck of the woods, so to speak, someone most likely very paramount in your community, a churchgoer, a business person, a civic leader, someone who has got some connections, has requested a little assistance from the heavy hitter. People who have pros on their payroll, people who take care of business when needed. You were a minor problem. Not a major job, simple. They, whoever they might be, simply underestimated you. Someone did not do their reconnaissance nor intel gathering on you at all."

Jim sat in his chair, both hands on his cup, looking down into his half-drunk coffee. Paul never said anything and rocked back again in his chair. Only the squeak was heard in the room.

"Okay," Jim finally stated. "It is time for me to leave. I will tell you this, Paul. I will be back in due time. I will be back to take care of the business. The point of fact is, several pieces of business. That is a promise. It will take a while to get things in order, but Paul, I am out of here."

"Will you need help getting where you want to go?"

"No, I do not think so. I will talk to you before we leave. It will be a while getting things in order."

"Jim, if you need anything, I mean anything..."

"Yes, I know. I really do appreciate the offer. As well as all the help you have given me over the years."

"Jim, I have some connections that can help in these matters."

"Paul, I am aware you do. However, well, we will see. Let me do some thinking and some planning. I have a lot to sift through. I just need time."

Paul interrupted. "James P., I"

Jim cut him off. "Paul, I really like the "Company," I do. I support them in all aspects. I really do not give a royal's fat rat's ass whether what they do is legal or illegal. However, it is the government. I hope you understand, nothing personal, okay. I know you used to work for them."

"Nothing personal taken. Jim, there are several things you are unaware of, but in due time my friend. Just remember there is no time limit."

Jim looked at Paul for a long minute. "Oh, you are talking about...then he stopped."

Then for the first time since he got into Paul's office, he broke a slight smile.

"Now, do you need any help moving?"

"No, Paul. I think I can handle all that myself. Besides, it would be best if you did not know exactly where I would relocate. No offense meant."

"Oh, believe me, I do understand."

"Well, I thought you might. Tell you what, let us say for the hell of it that I am somewhere in the northern part of Georgia, just in case, someone might ask. Okay."

"Hey, good enough for me." Then Paul smiled, got up from his squeaky chair, walked around his well-worn desk, and stuck his hand out. Jim rose as he approached, and they gripped each hand, grabbing the lower arm just above the wrist...and held it looking into each other's eyes. "For the five points," Paul stated. Jim repeated his words.

"Thanks, Paul. Thank you for everything. I owe you a lot."

"No, you don't owe me a damn thing. I will do some leg work for you, and when you are ready, the report will be ready."

James Patrick O'Francis would find a way to levy the justice he felt was just. After all that had happened in the past year, he and Dawn had already decided it was time for them to move from the area.

But James Patrick O'Francis would suffer through two more tragic events in his life before he was able to move from the area. These events would alter his life forever. He would never recover from the sudden loss of his youngest son Patrick and the unexpected death of his beloved wife. As a result, he would never live in the area again.

However, there was no time limit for the Irishman to seek retribution for the hardships that had been bestowed on him and his family. His list was long, he had an uncanny memory, and he never forgot. Fate would rule his future. And for many, only a mournful dirge would echo through the mountains.

So, Let It Be Said, So, Let It Be Written

Bruce had returned from his last trip to the south and had placed a call to Brian K. O'Francis. He informed him that all the Intel and recon had been done that could be done on the next mission.

Over two years, the missing or dead was up to five. The list had shrunk to the last three people that had been a significant player in the character assassination and the attempted assassination of James Patrick O'Francis and his wife. James Patrick took it personally when it came to his family's hardships. There was still looming the questionable death of his son Patrick.

James Patrick blamed the medical field for the sudden and unexpected death of his beloved "Twin Flame." Two doctors in particular. Again, there was nothing he could do about her death.

As for his adversaries, Jim knew how Dawn felt each time they came at him. As a result, James Patrick became more bitter and more withdrawn.

James Patrick requested from Brian K. specific ways each mission was to be carried out, and he and Vince honored his requests.

James P. and Brian K. had become close, and he had, in one of their earlier business meetings with Vince Spadalini, revealed to them his actual place of residence. Jim had misjudged both of them. Nevertheless, he was pleasantly surprised that they admired him for handling the entire sequence of events.

James Patrick had learned that Paul was an intricate part of the O'Francis/Spadalini business operations, making it much easier for him to be accepted by both men into their business world.

Dawn had died a few years before their planned move to the Big Sky Country, and James Patrick's bitterness ran more profound than ever toward the people who had driven him from their home in Virginia. A home they had spent thirty-plus years getting the way Dawn liked it. Dawn loves the little village and the place they had created at the foot of the mountains in Virginia. She had been such an intricate part of the design of the interior and the landscape surrounding their home, making it harder on James Patrick than he had imagined.

His coldness and calculations for planning and attention to the minuteness of details surprised Vince but not Brian, Bruce, or Paul. They knew how he had been trained and who he had served with. The elite was always meticulous regarding the details of any mission because their lives depended on it.

James Patrick had begun to enjoy the hotel business Brian had talked him into participating in. He learned to appreciate the involvement and association with the people he was getting to know in Brian's and Vince's worlds, which was a surprise to even himself. He learned that every one of Brian's extraordinary employees vetted and hired was like him, making it easy to work with. They all had the same mindset.

Carl Decal would be a special treat for James Patrick. The orchestration of Carl's ultimate demise was at J. Patrick's own hands at J. Patrick's request. Time was irrelevant. There is no time limit. Everyone pays the price for the injustice and suffering one may incur.

James Patrick O'Francis' entire life had flipped to the other side of the "pancake." A whole world far different from just a simple teacher, which was all he wanted to be. However, Fate?

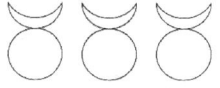

J. Michael O'Connor

Forever Young;

When I Dream; Eres TU

Time Is Up

Dream Weaver:

Singer/songwriter:

Gary Wright

Like a Rock

Bob Seger

Singer/songwriter

Forever Young

Rod Stewart; Lyrics; Bob Dylan

When I Dream: Crystal Gayle

Songwriter: Sandy Mason

Eres Tu

Lyrics: Juna Carlos Calderon De Arroyabe

Mocedades

J. Michael O'Connor

www.ingramcontent.com/pod-product-compliance
Lightning Source LLC
Chambersburg PA
CBHW071110250626
47159CB00002B/673